ODD
WEIRD &
LITTLE

Other Books by Patrick Jennings

Guinea Dog

Lucky Cap

Invasion of the Dognappers

My Homework Ate My Homework

Guinea Dog 2

Patrick Jennings

ODD
WEIRD&
LITTLE

EGMONT
USA
NEW YORK

EGMONT

We bring stories to life

First published by Egmont USA, 2014
443 Park Avenue South
New York, NY 10016

Copyright © 2014 by Patrick Jennings
All Rights Reserved
1 3 5 7 9 8 6 4 2

This novel is based on the short story "Odd, Weird, and Little," by Patrick Jennings, which originally appeared in *Storyworks* magazine, January 2009.

Library of Congress Cataloging-in-Publication Data

Jennings, Patrick.
Odd, weird & little / Patrick Jennings.
pages cm
Summary: Befriending a very strange new student, Toulouse, helps outsider Woodrow stand up to the class bullies who have been picking on them both.
ISBN 978-1-60684-374-1 (hardcover)
[1. Friendship—Fiction. 2. Eccentrics and eccentricities—Fiction.
3. Bullies—Fiction. 4. Middle schools—Fiction. 5. Schools—Fiction.]
I. Title.
PZ7.J4298715Odd 2014
[Fic]—dc23
2013018248

ISBN 978-1-60684-375-8 (eBook)

Printed in the United States of America

**For Peter and Tate,
Original, Wise, and Loopy**

Contents

ODD WEIRD & LITTLE

1. Our New Student

The new kid walks in.

"Excuse me, class," Mr. Logwood says. "Our new student has arrived. His name is Toulouse, and he just moved here from Quebec, which is a province of Canada. A province is like a state. His first language is French, but I'm told he's learning English quickly." He smiles down at the new boy.

None of us smile. We just stare at Toulouse.

He's short. Real short. Kindergartner short. And he's wearing a gray suit with thin black stripes. And a black tie. Tell me that isn't weird—a kid wearing a suit and tie to school. Plus, he's wearing tiny, round wire-rimmed glasses over his very large, round eyes. And an old-man hat. And black leather gloves.

And he's carrying a black briefcase. He kind of looks like my great-grandpa, only smaller. Way smaller.

This is an extremely weird kid. Definitely weirder than me. Probably the weirdest in our school. Maybe the weirdest on earth.

I glance over at Garrett Howell. He's grinning. Probably dreaming of terrible things to do to poor Toulouse.

I know what Garrett is capable of. I've been one of his victims for years now. Why? Maybe because I have orange hair and an overbite. I'm also clumsy, and sometimes I can't speak clearly, especially when I'm stressed. My words get all jammed up. I don't like dodgeball, tetherball, chasing games, or making fun of people. I do like to read books. I also keep lots of stuff in my pockets. I like to make things out of duck tape, and occasionally I wear things I make out of it: wristbands, bow ties, caps. . . . I insist on calling it *duck* tape, not *duct* tape, which is what most people call it. It was invented during World War II to waterproof ammunition. Waterproof. Duck. Duck tape.

I don't think any of this makes me weird. Compared to Toulouse, I'm practically normal.

"How ... do ... you ... pronounce ... your ... last ... name, Toulouse?" Mr. Logwood asks, as if pausing after every word will help the kid understand a foreign language. He writes Toulouse's full name on the whiteboard: "Toulouse Hulot."

Toulouse Hulot doesn't answer. He just stares.

"That's ... okay," Mr. Logwood says. "You ... can ... tell ... us ... later. Would ... you ... like ... to ... hang ... up ... your ... hat ... and ... coat?"

Toulouse shakes his head. Some of the kids giggle.

"That's ... fine," Mr. Logwood says, though you're not allowed to wear a hat indoors at our school.

Mr. Logwood leads Toulouse over to our group. Toulouse stares at us, one at a time, his head swiveling, his eyes frozen in their sockets. It's creepy.

"Toulouse will be in your group, people.

Please introduce yourselves and help him feel at home." Mr. Logwood turns and walks away.

"Hi, I'm Monique," Monique Whitlow says.

"Ursula," says Ursula Lowry.

"Garrett," Garrett says, sticking out his hand like he wants to shake.

His henchman, Hubcap Ostwinkle, whose real name is Vitus Ostwinkle, snickers.

Garrett's up to something. Joy buzzer? Death grip? Did he slobber into his palm? I would not put anything past the guy.

When Toulouse holds out his gloved hand, Garrett jerks his own back and runs his fingers smoothly through his stubbly hair. The fake-out handshake. Never funny.

I take Toulouse's hand and shake it. His glove is soft and sewn together with heavy black stitches. There's something strange about the way his hand feels inside it, as if it's too small, too light. His bones feel thin and fragile. I grip his hand gently, just in case.

"I'm . . . ," I say, then momentarily forget my name. "Woodrow Schwette?" I say it like a question.

Hubcap snorts like a donkey. *Donkey* is a polite word for what he is.

Toulouse makes a little bow in my direction. Which is odd, but also sort of classy.

He hops up onto his chair. His feet don't reach the floor.

"Name's Hubcap," Hubcap says. "You're really short, kid."

So rude.

"Please take out your writing notebooks, class," Mr. Logwood announces. "Today we are going to write about how it might feel to be a new student in a new classroom. Of course, Toulouse, you ... can ... write ... about ... how ... it ... *does* ... feel ... to ... be ... a ... new ... student."

Toulouse sets his briefcase on his desk, unsnaps its two silver buckles, and takes out a small, square black bottle, a white feather, and a book with a plain black cover. He unscrews the top of the bottle and dips the pointy end of the feather into it.

Monique and Ursula stare at him like he just climbed out of a flying saucer. Ursula actually points.

Toulouse opens the black book and begins writing. It must be a journal of some kind. The feather—a quill?—makes scratchy noises as he drags it across the paper. He stops every few words or so to redip.

Nobody else writes. We all watch him. He doesn't seem to notice. Or care.

No doubt about it: he's weird. But in a weirdly cool way.

2. Weirder Than Woody

At recess everyone is talking about Toulouse.

Everyone but me. I'm not talking to anyone, nor is anyone talking to me. They're all talking together by the swing set, and I'm hanging by my knees from the climbing structure next to them, the one that's a ladder that goes up, then bends horizontally, then bends back down, ending up on the ground again. Climb it and you end up no higher than you started. A pointless ladder. A ladder to nowhere.

I do listen, though.

Monique says, "He never speaks."

Ursula: "He doesn't speak *English*."

Monique: "He has a *briefcase*."

Ursula: "He keeps an *ink bottle* in his briefcase."

Garrett: "He wears a *suit*."

Hubcap: "Yeah! And a *tie*."

Ursula: "His eyes are *huge*."

Monique: "He's little."

Ursula: "He's odd."

Garrett: "He's seriously *weird*. Look at him!"

Hubcap: "Yeah, look at him!"

He points at a tree at the edge of the playground. Toulouse is perched on a high branch, reading.

I jump down from the Ladder to Nowhere and walk over to Toulouse's tree. He's holding an old hardcover book, the kind without a jacket. It looks enormous in his tiny lap.

"Excuse me? Toulouse?" I call to him. "I'm Woodrow? You know . . . from . . . I'm in your group?"

He looks up from his book and says, "Who?" It's the first word I've heard him say. His voice is whispery and hollow. Kind of ghostlike. Kind of flutey. Kind of spooky.

"Woodrow?" I say again. "I'm in . . . I sit next . . . you don't remember?"

He nods yes, then sits waiting for me to say

something else. The problem is that I don't have anything else. Striking up conversations is not something I'm good at.

So we stare at each other for a while.

Quite a while.

Then at last I think of something to say.

"I like your hat."

He nods thank you.

"What's that you're reading?" I ask. I'm warming up.

He turns the book toward me, though I'm not sure why. I can't possibly read its title from way down here.

"Is it good?"

He nods yes.

I run out of things to say again, so we go back to staring.

In time, the bell rings. Toulouse doesn't move.

"That means it's time to . . . you know . . . go in?"

I look away, point to the students all rushing to get in line. When I look back, he's not on his branch anymore. I gasp. I mean, the guy was really high. Did he fall?

No. He's standing next to me. How did he get down so fast?

We walk together toward the others. Toulouse comes up to my elbow, even with his hat on.

"Hey, Woody!" Garrett howls. "I think you finally found someone weirder than you!"

He always calls me Woody. He's the only one who does, except Hubcap, who repeats everything Garrett says.

"Yeah, Woody!" Hubcap echoes. "Even weirder than you!"

Toulouse seems calm, like being insulted doesn't bother him. I've lived in this country since I was born, and have gone to Uwila Elementary since kindergarten, and I still get upset when Garrett taunts me. I'm impressed how Toulouse doesn't let him ruffle his feathers.

"Ignore them," I whisper.

"Who?" he says.

"Exactly," I say.

3. Learning to Watercolor

After recess is art. Ms. Wolf sets a big basket filled with fruit and flowers on a stool in the center of the room—a still life, she calls it— and we sit in a circle and paint it.

She's been trying to show us how to use watercolors properly. She says we shouldn't swirl our brushes in the plastic jar of water then go straight to the tiny hockey pucks of paint. That just makes a mess and blends all the colors into a dull, dark purplish-brown. What we're supposed to do is dip the tip of our brush into the water, dab away most of the water on a piece of paper towel, go to the pucks for paint, then mix it on the plastic plate with the little compartments. Once we have the color we want, we brush it on the paper.

For most of us, though, the fun isn't in painting the fruit and flowers. It's in swirling our brushes in the jar of water and watching the colors change, then slopping the water onto the pucks and watching the paint run and mix. The fun is in making a sloppy, colorful mess.

Most of our paintings are dark purplish-brown puddles. Our sheets of paper are soaked and pucker and start to peel. But we don't mind. We're expressing ourselves, which Ms. Wolf is always telling us we should do. We express ourselves in messes.

Ms. Wolf hurries around the classroom in her apron, complaining. "No, no, that's too much! . . . Easy does it! . . . One color at a time! . . . Get more paper towels! Quickly!"

In the middle of this chaos, I notice Toulouse, sitting off by himself, next to the window. There isn't enough room for an extra kid at the tables. We have a big class.

Toulouse's paper is sitting upright on a little wooden tripod, an easel, that he got out of his briefcase. Who carries an easel in a briefcase? Who carries an easel, period? Or a briefcase?

Toulouse carefully dips his brush into the jar of water, dabs it on a folded paper towel, touches the tip to one of the color pucks, mixes it in one of the plastic plate compartments, then paints. I can't see his picture from where I'm sitting, and we're not supposed to get out of our seats. I'd really like to see it, but rules are rules.

When it's nearly time to go, Ms. Wolf says, "Okay, class, please begin cleaning up. *Carefully.*"

All of us stop painting at once and dunk our brushes deep into the jars to clean them. We swish them violently. Hubcap knocks over the one on our table. Ursula squeals. Monique snatches her painting and holds it over her head so it won't get wet. I doubt a little water could make it look any worse.

We are now allowed to leave our seats, but only to carry our paintings over to the windowsill and lay them out to dry. After I do, I walk over to Toulouse. He's carefully drying his brushes with sheets of paper towel.

"I love your easel," I say, then glance at his painting. It is so good! You can actually see the pears and apples and the pink flowers and the basket they're sitting in. They look almost real. Not like a photograph, though. They look realer.

"Toulouse!" I say, then can't think of anything else to say.

"Look at Toulouse's painting!" Monique says.

The noise level in the room drops, and people start wandering over.

"Keep cleaning up now!" Ms. Wolf says, clapping her hands. "We're not finished! Clean up, please!"

"Ms. Wolf!" Monique says. "You have to come see Toulouse's painting!"

"Later, Monique," Ms. Wolf says. She picks up two Mason jars of water, one in each hand. "Everyone now! Please keep cleaning up!"

"But Ms. Wolf," Ursula says, after she's looked at Toulouse's painting, "you really should look. It's *amazing*."

"Ursula, you really should be *cleaning*," Ms. Wolf replies. "I'll look at it after we've finished."

No one is listening to her. Everyone has

slowly gathered around Toulouse's picture. When Ms. Wolf sees this, she stomps over, sloshing the water in the jars she's holding.

"Really, children, you need to be—"

She sees Toulouse's painting. Her mouth falls open, and the jars of dark purplish-brown water crash to the floor.

4. Outside

"Did you see his painting?" Monique asks Ursula on the playground after lunch. Ursula and Monique are swinging on swings.

Ursula: "Yes. It was a masterpiece. Like a Rembrandt."

Monique: "More like a Matisse."

Hubcap: "What's that?"

Ursula: "Don't you remember? Ms. Wolf showed us paintings of his. The ones with the fruit?"

Garrett: "I don't get painting fruit. By the time you finish it, it's rotten and you can't eat it."

Hubcap: "Right! This Matisse guy must have wasted a lot of food!"

Monique: "The fruit was plastic."

Ursula: "So were the flowers."

Monique: "Toulouse's painting was as good as Matisse's."

Ursula: "I don't know. Matisse was a great artist. Toulouse is just a kid."

Garrett: "Just a *weird* kid."

Hubcap: "Exactly. Weird."

Monique: "You're just jealous."

Garrett: "Jealous? Of being able to paint fruit?"

Hubcap: "Who wants to paint fruit?"

Garrett: "Not me."

Hubcap: "Me, neither."

Ursula: "Did you see Toulouse hop up on the supply cabinet?"

Garrett: "Yeah, the scaredy-cat."

Hubcap: "Scaredy-cat! Afraid of a little water!"

Monique: "He wasn't afraid. He was protecting his painting."

Garrett: "He was chicken."

Monique: "Which is he: a chicken or a cat?"

Hubcap: "Both! Right, Garrett?"

Garrett: "Yeah, both. Plus, he's weird."

Ursula: "Maybe he's a genius."

Garrett: "A genius? How can he be a genius when he can't even talk?"

Hubcap: "Yeah! He can't even talk!"

Ursula: "He can talk. He just can't speak *English*."

Garrett: "And what kind of name is Toulouse? 'To *lose*,' more like."

Hubcap: "Yeah! 'To be a loser'! Right, Garrett?"

Garrett: "Right. Let's play some tetherball, Hub."

Hubcap: "Lead the way."

They walk away, laughing and punching and elbowing each other.

Monique and Ursula keep swinging. Monique glances up at me as she reaches my height. I'm sitting on the Ladder to Nowhere, eavesdropping.

"Maybe they, like . . . ," I say. "Maybe in Quebec . . . they teach watercolor . . . teach kids how to . . . you know . . . paint . . . really young . . . maybe in kindergarten," I say.

Monique shrugs, glances away, then, having hit the peak of her swing, drops backward and away.

5. Walking Up a Tree

I climb down from the Ladder and walk over to Toulouse's tree.

I have to tilt my head to see him. He's sitting on the same branch with his briefcase open in his lap. He peeks around it and looks down at me. Ursula's right about one thing: he has huge eyes. Even from this distance they're weirdly big.

"Hi," I say.

"Who?" he says.

Maybe *who* is *hi* in French?

"It's me, Woodrow. Can I come up?"

He stares a few seconds, long enough to make me feel uneasy, then blinks a couple of times. Is that a yes?

I reach up for the lowest branch, but it's

too high. I hop for it. Nope. How did Toulouse reach it?

I pull some cord out of my pocket. It's good to keep some nylon cord with you. You never know when it will come in handy. I have a coil of about four feet in length. I found this piece in our backyard. It's probably part of somebody's old clothesline. It's pale yellow and fraying, but it's still strong.

I tie one end around a flat stone, then fling it up at the branch. It passes over and swings back down and conks me in the forehead. I see stars for a while, but then I'm all right.

I untie the stone and wrap the ends of the cord around my hands a few times, then tug them till they're taut, and begin walking up the tree trunk, Batman-style. The bark is slipperier than I thought it'd be, though. I try walking faster, but I get no higher. I'm speed skating horizontally on a tree trunk. Meanwhile, the cord tightens and starts cutting into my hands. Above me, where it's rubbing against the branch, it starts to split. Finally, it snaps, and I fall to the ground. I land on my back with a thud.

I don't see stars. I see leaves, branches, and bits of sky. I think you see stars only when you get hit on the head. The fall knocked the air out of me, though. I just stay flat on my back, close my eyes, and wait for my breath to return.

"Woodrow?"

He knows my name.

I open my eyes, and he's standing right next to me. How does he do that?

"I'm all right," I tell him. "Well, not *all* right . . . but I'm . . . I'm not badly injured or anything."

His head tilts slightly, like he's confused.

"I fall all the time," I say. "My body's . . . used to it."

I'm lucky I fell on my back, since most of the stuff I'm carrying is stuffed into my front pockets. The metal pencil sharpener, for example, and a couple of small rolls of duck tape, an empty mint tin, and a Ticonderoga, which is my favorite pencil. I do have one roll of red duck tape in my back pocket, however, which didn't feel good to land on.

Toulouse reaches out a gloved hand. He's

holding his briefcase in his other one.

I gently take his hand and pretend to let him pull me to a sitting position. I doubt he could do it. He's pretty short.

"Thanks. Sorry I . . . you know . . . interrupted your lunch." I point at his case.

He just stares, like he doesn't understand what I'm saying.

"Your . . . lunch?" I say. Now I sound like Mr. Logwood. I pretend I'm eating by moving my hand to my mouth and making biting and chewing motions. "Lunch? Meal? Food? I'm sorry?"

He lets go of my hand and takes a watch from his pocket that is attached to his vest by a chain. He squeezes it, and the brass cover pops open, which is cool. He reads the time and nods, then snaps the watch shut and slips it back in his pocket. He looks at the building.

The bell rings.

I get to my feet and try to reach around to brush the dirt off my back. Toulouse removes a little whisk broom from inside his jacket and helps me out. The guy has cool stuff.

"Thanks," I say.

He stops brushing and puts the whisk broom back in his coat.

"Your still life was . . ." I can't think of the right word to describe what I think his painting was. It was amazing, beautiful, and surprising. Is there one word for all that?

He stares at me. I swear his eyes are as big and round as the roll of tape in my back pocket.

"It was . . . you know . . . it was super-something . . . not super-duper . . . super . . . um . . . uh . . . su*perb*?"

He gives me a little bow. He understands.

I bow back.

6. Logwood Sings

"Ms. . . . Wolf . . . tells . . . me . . . you . . . are . . . quite . . . the . . . artist," Mr. Logwood says to Toulouse when we're back in the classroom.

Toulouse doesn't answer.

"He's an *amazing* artist," Monique says. "You should see his painting."

"Of fruit," Garrett says under his breath.

Hubcap snickers.

"Respect, gentlemen," Mr. Logwood says. "Do you need me to sing it for you?"

"No!" Garrett and Hubcap say in unison.

The song Mr. Logwood sings is an old one my parents listen to sometimes. Mr. Logwood doesn't sing very well, though.

"Then please get out your math materials while I collect some for Toulouse."

"Who?" Toulouse says at the mention of his name.

Garrett and Hubcap snicker.

Mr. Logwood begins singing the old song.

"Okay! Sorry! *Sorry!*" Garrett says.

Hubcap: "Yeah, we're *so* sorry!"

Mr. Logwood ends the song. "Math materials, gentlemen," he says, then gets some for Toulouse.

We've been studying shapes. Triangles. Polygons. Quadrilaterals. When Toulouse gets today's handout, which is called, "Greater Than Right: Obtuse Angles," he opens his briefcase and takes out: a steel ruler with etched markings and a cork backing; a steel protractor (also etched); a pink rubber eraser; and three yellow, unsharpened pencils (Ticonderogas!). I dig the sharpener out of my pocket. It's a heavy, bronze cylinder (speaking of geometric shapes . . .) about an inch in diameter with a sharp metal blade on the top. I love it, and I'm hoping Toulouse will appreciate its fine workmanship.

"Would you like this . . . to use?" I ask him. "The one on the wall . . . it's terrible. It mangles your Ticonderogas."

He stares at me.

Too much English?

I hold the sharpener out and smile.

He sticks out his gloved hand, palm up. I set the sharpener in it. He bounces his hand, weighing it, then he picks it up with the gloved fingers of his other hand and inspects it. One of his eyes close, and I notice a strange thing: just before his eyelids touch, a dark diagonal line appears between them, over his large iris. Does he wear contacts?

When he's finished looking the sharpener over—I can tell he appreciates the workmanship—he slides one of his pencils into the smaller of the two sharpening ports and twists it. The painted skin of the Ticonderoga curls over the blade like an apple peel.

I dig into my other pocket and take out the small, empty mint tin, then pop it open with my thumb. It still smells of peppermint.

"For the shavings," I say.

He nods and shakes the shavings loose. They flutter down into the tin.

"This is so sweet," Garrett says.

"Touching," Hubcap adds.

"Two dorks in love."

"Dork love."

Garrett makes a little kissing sound. Hubcap joins in.

I suddenly wonder whether being friendly to Toulouse is such a good idea. Garrett claims Toulouse is weirder than me. If I become friends with him, what will that say about me? If I distance myself from Toulouse, maybe Garrett will finally leave me alone.

Toulouse lowers his hands and stares at Garrett's puckering mouth, then pivots his head and stares at Hubcap's.

"Stop staring at me, freak," Hubcap says, squirming.

Toulouse makes a sound with his mouth. I think he's trying to make a kissing sound, but it ends up sounding more clicky than kissy.

"I think he wants a kiss, Hub," Garrett says.

Hubcap: "Well, he's not getting one."

"Leave him alone, Garrett," Monique says.

I was going to say that, but it got stuck in my throat.

Toulouse hands the sharpener back to me with a thank-you nod, then takes a small notepad with a brown leather cover out of his briefcase and flips it open. He scribbles something on the pad, tears off the sheet, and passes it to Garrett.

We all lean in to read it. In fancy cursive, it reads:

Avoid obtuseness.

7. Obtuse

So he knows some English. Some pretty fancy English, actually.

Maybe he's only learned to read and write it, though. Maybe he can't speak it.

Obtuse is on our math handout: "Greater Than Right: Obtuse Angles." It's an angle greater than ninety degrees but less than one hundred eighty. That is, it's between a right angle and a straight line.

I'm pretty sure that's not what Toulouse meant by *obtuseness*, though. Maybe he's being clever. Maybe the word has other meanings.

During Silent Sustained Reading, I look it up in the dictionary. It lists two meanings for *obtuse*. One is about angles. The other definition is "blunt or dull." Toulouse was telling Garrett to avoid dullness, to be sharp, which Garrett definitely wasn't being.

Toulouse is the sharp one.

I go back to my seat. Everybody's reading. Monique's book is called *The Witch Family*. Ursula's is *Calling on Dragons*. Garrett's is a nonfiction picture book about weapons called *Arms and Armor*. Hubcap is flipping through another in the same series. It's called *Combat*. Toulouse is reading the same book he had in the tree, which is called *Nonsense Songs, Stories, Botany, and Alphabets*. Botany?

He has the book lying on his desk, so I can see there are drawings in it. Cartoons. Black-and-white line drawings. They look goofy, like the ones in my book. (I'm reading Captain Underpants, the one about the teacher who gives wedgies.) The words in Toulouse's book are in English, which doesn't surprise me, since the title is in English, too.

Toulouse also has a small, paperback French/English dictionary on his desk, which he took out of his briefcase. That case sure holds a lot of stuff.

I try to focus on my book, but I can't seem to stop spying on Toulouse. He reads with his eyes opened so wide it's like he's watching a scary movie. And his eyes don't move left to right when he reads. They stare straight ahead. His head moves instead. When he finishes a line, his head snaps back to the beginning.

He laughs a couple of times—just little hoots—then he quickly covers his mouth with his hand and glances around to see if anyone noticed. Both times, I dive behind my book. I don't fool him the second time. He waits for me to come out, then he spins his book around and slides it toward me.

On the page is a drawing of some round-faced kids aboard a circular boat with a white flag flying from a mast in the center. It's sailing in a choppy sea, and some of the kids have their hands up in the air, like they're excited. The others look angry, or worried.

Under the drawing is a poem. It's called "The Jumblies." These Jumbly people went to sea in a sieve. I'm pretty sure a sieve is like a colander, something you use to drain liquid, like from pasta or beans. A bowl filled with holes, in other words. No wonder some of them look worried, or angry.

The poem rhymes, which seems babyish to me, and has a chorus at the end of each verse about how the Jumblies have green heads and blue hands, which is sort of funny but also kind of babyish. I figure if I was learning a new language, I might have to read books like this. But Toulouse understands words like *obtuseness*. This book must be too basic for him, so he must read it because he likes it.

I look at him and smile politely. Then I open my book to a particularly funny page and slide it to him. I feel a little bad that mine is so much funnier, but this is America, and he might as well get used to how good things can be here.

He stares down at the book.

And stares.

And stares.

Amazingly, he doesn't laugh. Maybe he doesn't get the humor. Maybe what's funny in Quebec and what's funny here are different.

He turns the page and keeps staring. A

minute later, he flips to the next page. Then the next one. Then he looks up at me. And hoots. I jump. Everyone jumps. It wasn't that loud a hoot. It's just that SSR time is pretty quiet.

He looks a little worried, like one of the Jumblies in the boat.

I probably should have warned him how funny the book is.

8. Wire, Feathers, and Hooks

Toulouse obviously loves Otto and Billy Bob, our goldfish.

They live on the windowsill next to Mr. Logwood's desk in a classic fishbowl: round, but flat on the sides, not spherical. (This geometry stuff is really sinking in.) They must be so bored. They putter around the bowl, fluttering their fins, passing each other without seeming to notice, or care. Now and then Otto will chase Billy Bob around, nipping at his tail fin.

I wonder if they like each other. Or hate each other. I think about being stuck in a glass bowl with Garrett. That would be more awful than the most awful thing in the universe. Well, unless Hubcap was in there, too.

If I had to be cooped up in a fishbowl forever with someone, I'd prefer it be Toulouse.

It's funny I feel this way, considering I just met him this morning. I guess so far I like him. It seems as if he likes me. It'd be great to have a friend, but I don't know if he would be such a great choice. Weird plus weird might make us double weird. Or triple. I'd get picked on, he'd get picked on, we'd get picked on—and by both Garrett and Hubcap. So that would be double triple. Six times the taunting. I should probably back off befriending Toulouse.

I mean, look at him. He's been staring at the fish so long that he's starting to attract attention. Lots of kids are watching him watch. I guess he really likes fish. Some people do.

For example, me. I'm not interested in goldfish in a bowl. It's depressing. But I like to catch them. I like fishing. What I really like doing is making lures and flies. I like assembling the wire and feathers and hooks.

We're supposed to be writing a chapter summary of the book we read during SSR, but I whisper, "Do you like to fish?"

He jumps and makes a peep sound.

"Sorry," I say. "I just saw ... noticed ... you're staring ..."

Toulouse nods but continues to stare at the fishbowl.

"So do you like to fish?" I ask.

He nods again.

"Do you make your own lures?"

Another nod.

"Do you own a rod ... tackle?"

He turns his head slowly and stares at me. Do his eyes *ever* move in their sockets? Maybe something is wrong with them. I probably shouldn't ask till I get to know him better.

"Oui," he says.

He definitely understands a lot more English than Mr. Logwood gives him credit for. I don't understand any French, but I know *oui* means yes.

He opens his briefcase and reaches inside. He's taken so much stuff out of it, I half expect him to pull out a floor lamp, like Mary Poppins did in the movie, but all he takes out is a small, gray, metal, hinged case. A case in a case. He opens the metal clasp. Inside are feathers, fur, hooks, fishing line, wire, and various tools. The case is a tackle box! He lifts out a perfect dragonfly with a glittering blue-sequined body.

I reach my hand up and close my mouth. I guess it fell open. I can't believe what I'm seeing. I've met a couple of kids who make lures and flies. I've never met one who carries tackle around with him.

Is there no way he and I can become friends? Curse you, Garrett Howell! You, too, Hubcap Ostwinkle!

Toulouse hands me the dragonfly, and, after looking around for Mr. Logwood (he's talking with a kid on the other side of the room), I take it. It's really fine work. Strong and beautiful. I wish I could try it out on real fish. I wish I was at the creek right now with Toulouse and our rods.

"We should go . . . do . . . do you want . . . I think we . . . ," I stammer. "There's a creek . . . we could . . . you know . . . fish at?"

He stares at me. No surprise there. But

he stares long enough this time that I begin to wonder if he's trying to think of some way to get out of going fishing with me without hurting my feelings. Then I wonder if he understood me. I mean, sure, he understands English okay, but was what I said really English?

I try again.

"Want to go fishing sometime?"

He stares.

I take this as a no. "Or not . . . no, you're probably . . . maybe you don't . . ."

"Okay," he says, a bit too loudly.

"Hey, he spoke," Monique says.

"Whoa," Garrett says. "He knows a whole word in English."

"Yeah, one whole word," Hubcap says.

I want to point out that Toulouse has also said "who" and my name, but I don't.

"Is that all you can say, little guy?" Garrett asks Toulouse. "Just one word?"

Toulouse stares at him. He blinks. Slowly. I see those funny diagonal lines flash in his eyes again.

"Yes," he says in his flutey little voice. "I can speak only the one."

Whether we become friends or not, I really like this guy.

9. Ladder to Nowhere

Toulouse and I sit on top of the Ladder to Nowhere during afternoon recess, making lures. He has terrific tools in his little tackle box: tweezers, needles, needle-nose pliers, superglue, and wire cutters. He shows me how to make the dragonfly, and I promise to show him how to make a grasshopper with an orange abdomen, which is one of my specialties.

Garrett and Hubcap walk up. Here comes the taunting times six.

"You guys making pretty jewelry?" Garrett asks, looking up at us.

Hubcap: "Pretty bracelets, maybe, to give each other on Valentine's Day?"

"It's October," I say.

"But you guys are in love, right?" Garrett

says, then starts singing, "'Woody and Weirdy . . . sitting in a tree . . .'"

Hubcap laughs, then chimes in.

Toulouse looks at me, confused.

If kids don't sing this song in Quebec, I want to move to Quebec.

"'. . . then comes Woody in a baby carriage,'" they finish, then bust up laughing.

"Isn't it supposed to be 'with a baby carriage'?" Ursula asks. She's swinging next to the Ladder. "I mean, is Woodrow the baby or the mom?"

"Does it matter?" Garrett asks.

Hubcap: "Maybe both!"

He reaches up and grabs a loose thread hanging from Toulouse's kit, twirls it around his finger a few times, then tugs it. The spool it's attached to bounces out of the kit. Toulouse strains to catch it, loses his balance, and starts falling forward. I reach out for him and end up slipping off the rung I'm sitting on. I catch myself with my knees, but my back slams against the rung behind me. I hook the bar with my arms. I'm stuck like a crab going down a drain, my arms and legs flailing.

Toulouse's kit and briefcase fall and land in the sand. Garrett and Hubcap pounce on them.

I look around for Toulouse, but he's no longer on the Ladder. He's also not below me on the ground. I scan the playground. There he is, perched atop the swing set, over Ursula's head. How'd he get up there? And so fast?

He sits there, watching Garrett and Hubcap as they go through his things. He's too polite, I think, to complain. Or maybe too scared.

I feel angry. Really angry. It's bad enough when Garrett and Hubcap are mean to me, but it stinks when they pick on poor little Toulouse. I can't not do something.

I unhook my arms and drop through the rungs till I'm hanging upside down from my knees, right above Garrett. I swing my arm down and snatch the handle of the briefcase, which causes it to slam shut. Garrett pulls his fingers out just in time. Too bad. I pull myself back up to safety. It was a daring and successful rescue operation, carried out fairly flawlessly.

I don't know where I found the bravery and flair, but I'm happy I did.

"Give that back!" Garrett says, jumping to his feet.

Hubcap leaps up and orders me to give it back, too. He's holding Toulouse's tackle box in his hand.

"Put that . . . ," I say. "That doesn't belong . . . Put it down!"

"It doesn't belong to you, either," Garrett says.

Hubcap: "Yeah!"

"Hey, where'd Weirdy go?" Garrett asks, looking around.

Hubcap: "Yeah. Where'd Loser go?"

I try not to look at the swing set.

The bell rings. I'm saved by it.

Hubcap drops the tackle box, then gives it a kick. The two of them then run off toward the building.

I drop to the ground. The tackle box is still closed. It's not dented or anything. I dust it off on my pant leg.

"Merci," Toulouse says.

I scream. How did he get here so fast?

"What did you say?" I ask.

"*Merci,*" he repeats. "Thank you."

"Oh. How do you say 'you're welcome' in French?"

"*De rien.*"

I repeat it the best I can.

"Good!" he says.

"*Merci,*" I say.

10. Ottoless

"So . . . Toulouse," Mr. Logwood says when we're back inside, "I've . . . noticed . . . you . . . like . . . the . . . goldfish. Would . . . you . . . like . . . to . . . feed . . . them?"

Toulouse nods enthusiastically, then hustles over on his short legs to the window beside Mr. Logwood's desk. The bowl is at his eye level. He presses his pointy little nose against the glass. I hear a clink. Must be his glasses.

Mr. Logwood hands him the fish food.

"We . . . give . . . them . . . two . . . shakes," he says.

I wonder if I should tell him he doesn't need to speak slowly to Toulouse, that Toulouse understands.

Nah, he's a teacher, he'll figure it out.

After giving Toulouse the fish food shaker, Mr. Logwood gets a step stool from the supply closet, but by the time he returns with it, Toulouse has hopped up onto the windowsill. We're not allowed on the windowsills.

Mr. Logwood laughs uncomfortably. "Okay. I . . . don't . . . usually . . . allow . . . students . . . up . . . there. Promise . . . you . . . will . . . be . . . careful?"

Toulouse doesn't answer. He leans his face over the fishbowl. His nose is practically touching the water. His eyes are opened very wide. He shakes some fish flakes into the bowl. They float on the surface. Usually Otto and Billy Bob rush up to eat them, but not this time. They swim in panicky circles at the bottom of the bowl.

The whole class is watching, spellbound.

"Okay," Mr. Logwood says. "Thank . . . you, Toulouse."

He holds out his hand. Is it for the shaker or to help Toulouse down? Toulouse does not need help getting down, that's for sure, but Mr. Logwood doesn't know that.

Toulouse hands him the fish food shaker, still not taking his eyes off the fish. He does not jump down from the windowsill.

Mr. Logwood coughs, then turns to us. "I believe we have a spelling test planned for now."

Garrett groans.

"Do I need to sing the respect song for you, Mr. Howell?" Mr. Logwood asks.

"No, no," Garrett says, painting a smile on his face. "I'd love to take a spelling test, Mr. Logwood."

He really doesn't like it when Mr. Logwood sings.

None of us are paying much attention to this conversation. For one thing, we've all heard it a million times. For another, Toulouse is still leaning over the fishbowl, gazing down at the frightened Otto and Billy Bob.

Sensing that everyone is staring at Toulouse, Mr. Logwood leans over and whispers in his ear, "Please . . . take . . . your . . . seat . . . now."

Toulouse doesn't move. He doesn't want to take his seat. He doesn't want to leave the fish. He likes the fish. Maybe he wants to catch them. He likes fishing. He makes his own lures. He carries a tackle box around with him.

But he wouldn't want to catch Otto and Billy Bob, would he? He wouldn't *eat* them? I mean, they're *gold*fish. They're pets.

I stand up and walk over to him.

"Come on," I say. "Come sit down."

Garrett snickers, then Hubcap does. Toulouse and I may as well go ahead and be friends now. That's how Garrett and Hubcap see us. And they're loving it.

"That's enough of that, boys," Mr. Logwood says in his deep, no-nonsense voice. "It's not easy adjusting to a new culture. We need to be compassionate and welcoming." He turns to me. "As Woodrow is being. Thank you, Woodrow."

I gesture "you're welcome" by lifting one shoulder then dropping it. I hook Toulouse's arm and give it a tug. He's as light as a feather. I lead him back to our desks.

"'K-I-S-S-I-N-G . . . ,'" Hubcap whisper-sings out of the corner of his mouth.

"Vitus," Mr. Logwood says. "I'm going to

need you to take a Think Time at the back of the room, please."

Hubcap jumps up and moves through the desks, pretending he doesn't care—grinning, fake-gagging, eye-rolling—but it's obvious he's embarrassed.

I don't get Hubcap, or Garrett. It's like they go out of their way to be mean, like they're proud of getting in trouble.

Toulouse and I sit down. I doubt Toulouse will have to take the spelling test. He didn't get the word list Mr. Logwood handed out yesterday. I didn't study it much, but I do remember it had tricky words with *i-e* or *e-i*: *believe, deceive, neighbor, seize....*

"*Oh!*" Ursula screams. She points at the fishbowl. "Where's Otto?"

11. Weirdness Factor

Everyone stares at Toulouse. He stares back, at one person at a time, in that odd, wide-eyed, head-pivoting way of his. He looks at the kids sitting behind him by twisting his head all the way around without turning his body. This adds to his weirdness factor. I don't think anyone is breathing.

We had all watched him gape at the fish. We'd all seen how he refused to walk away from them. No one claims they saw him touch Otto. We had all been distracted by Hubcap getting a Think Time. I had been standing right next to Toulouse. I didn't see him get up from his chair. But I was distracted by Hubcap, too. Not for long, but, knowing how fast Toulouse can move, it could have been long enough for him to ... to ...

But he couldn't have. He just *couldn't*. He isn't wet in the slightest. Wouldn't his gloves be wet? They aren't.

Besides, why would he steal a fish from a fishbowl?

"Did . . . you . . . see . . . what . . . happened . . . to . . . Otto?" Mr. Logwood asks Toulouse in a soft, patient voice.

Toulouse stares at him.

"Otto!" Ursula says. "You know, our *fish*!"

"He doesn't speak English," someone says.

"Yes, he does," Garrett says. "I heard him say a lot of English words."

Everybody starts whispering.

"Quiet, please," Mr. Logwood says, raising a hand. "Toulouse, is this true?" he says without any pauses. "Can you understand me?"

All the attention has caused Toulouse to sink down in his chair, which makes him look even smaller. He gives a tiny nod.

"See?" Garrett snarls. "He understands English good enough."

"*Well* enough," Monique says.

Mr. Logwood coughs. He always does this

when he's preparing to redirect our attention. "Time for the spelling test. Clear your desks. Get out a sheet of writing paper and something to write with, please."

Everyone groans. Everyone, that is, except Toulouse. He sighs. Is he relieved?

"But what about Otto?" Ursula asks.

"We'll deal with that later," Mr. Logwood says without looking at her. "It's time for spelling."

He leans over Toulouse, and says quietly, "Obviously, you can't take the test. Please wait for me over there, in the Gathering Place, and I'll bring you the list. You can follow along as I read the words aloud."

Toulouse hops down from his chair and heads toward the Gathering Place, an area with a circular rug for us students and a short, stuffed armchair for Mr. Logwood. It's where we sit and share.

Toulouse hops into the chair. There's a loud gasp.

"Actually, Toulouse," Mr. Logwood says with a strained smile, "that chair is reserved for me."

Toulouse climbs down and sits on the rug.

Mr. Logwood hands him a list of the spelling words. Toulouse stands up and looks around, as if he lost something. Then he starts walking back toward his desk. I see why: he forgot his briefcase. It's on the floor by his chair.

"Where are you going, Toulouse?" Mr. Logwood asks.

"He forgot his briefcase," I say.

"I see," Mr. Logwood says, then to us, asks, "Are we ready? Let's begin the test. The first word is *weird*."

We all start writing. *Weird* sure is a weird word. It breaks the *i* before *e* rule. It should be spelled *wierd*.

When I finish writing it and look up, Toulouse is back in the Gathering Place with his briefcase. I didn't notice him pick it up, or even come near his desk. The kid moves so silently.

"Hey!" Ursula says, pointing. "He's back! Otto's back in the bowl!"

12. Latin

After spelling, we go to choir. We walk single file down the hall, Mr. Logwood in the lead, then Toulouse, then me and the rest of our class, which means everyone is whispering about Toulouse behind his back. I've done enough dumb stuff in the past to know how that feels, like the time I pretended to be a badger and put chopsticks in my mouth and ended up with them jammed down my throat. Everyone whispered behind my back for a couple of days after that one.

Not that Toulouse did a dumb thing. I don't know what he did, and neither does anyone else. I admit it's suspicious, but there's no proof he had anything to do with Otto's disappearance. Or reappearance.

Unfortunately, getting judged for things you didn't do is part of life for a kid who gets picked on.

I feel bad for Toulouse. I want to show him that not everyone thinks he's a freak. But we're supposed to walk single file and not talk. And let's face it: for once I'm not the class freak. That's a good thing. Right?

When we enter the music room, Mr. Weldon pounces on us, as usual.

"Take your seats at once!" he shouts, then dabs his face with his white handkerchief. The guy is always sweating. This is probably because: one, he is always worked up, and, two, he always wears long-sleeved white shirts buttoned up to his throat with a skinny black tie that swings like a pendulum as he dabs his face with his hanky. He also wears a black vest, and black pants, and shiny black ankle-high boots. No wonder he sweats.

"No monkey business!" he practically shouts. "That means you, Vitus! Stop your stomping. Sit down! No pushing, Garrett! The risers are quite dangerous! There is to be no pushing, *any*one! I am not in the mood for monkey business! Are you listening, Garrett? I hope so, because I am not fooling around today. Sit down and be completely qui—!"

He stops mid-word when he sees Toulouse.

"Why, who are you, kind sir? Aren't you a dapper young man!"

"Dapper!" Garrett laughs behind his hand. Hubcap snickers.

"Quiet!" Mr. Weldon snaps, whirling on them. "Quiet or I will give you a *solo* to sing."

Garrett shuts his mouth. Hubcap, too. If there's anything they dislike more than Mr. Logwood singing, it's having to sing themselves.

Mr. Weldon returns to Toulouse. "What is your name, young man?"

Toulouse stares at Mr. Weldon, speechless. He bows.

Mr. Weldon laughs. "Such a young gentleman! I love this boy!" He returns the bow.

Garrett and Hubcap try to hold it in but fail. They burst into laughter.

"Think Time!" Mr. Weldon roars at them.

"Both of you! Go and think! It will do you a world of good!"

I like Mr. Weldon. He scares me a little with all the sweating and whirling and roaring, but he sees right through Garrett and Hubcap, and sets them straight.

"His name is Toulouse," I say. "He's from Quebec."

"Ah!" Mr. Weldon says, wagging his finger at the ceiling. "*Oui, oui!* So it's *Monsieur* Toulouse! *Enchanté!* A great pleasure to meet you, monsieur. And welcome! *Bienvenue!* Please, have a seat and we will begin our musical lesson for today, which I hope you will find to your liking!"

Toulouse bows again and sits down. Mr. Weldon has cheered him up. Nothing like being treated special to lift your spirits.

The past few weeks we've been working on songs for the holiday concert in December. I've never heard of any of the songs Mr. Weldon is making us perform. We have no normal holiday songs, like "Jingle Bells" or "Frosty the Snowman." One is in Latin and dates from the someteenth century. We just sing *"dona nobis pacem"* over and over and over. It means "give us peace."

Mr. Weldon stands in front of us, takes a deep breath, raises his arms, then signals for us to start. We sing the song all the way through, with him mouthing it and making all sorts of hand gestures that mean louder or softer or faster or slower.

"Not too bad," Mr. Weldon says afterward. "From the top again, but this time, everyone sing, please, and with feeling. Monsieur Toulouse, would you like to join us?"

Toulouse nods.

"Excellent!" Mr. Weldon says. "And Garrett and Vitus, please return to the group, and please comport yourself like gentlemen."

They walk over and step up onto the risers without stomping.

We sing the song again.

"Bravo!" Mr. Weldon says. "Much better! And Toulouse, you sing like a bird."

I was thinking a flute, but his singing is kind of birdlike.

"A cuckoo," Garrett whispers to Hubcap, who snickers.

"Out!" Mr. Weldon says. "Out of my classroom. Go to the office, both of you. Such insolence!"

Mr. Weldon gets teased more than any of our teachers, but, like Toulouse, he doesn't seem to care much. He's a busy guy and can't spend all his energy trying to make everyone happy, or trying to be cool. Some teachers do that. They say "awesome" and give high fives. But Mr. Weldon doesn't pretend to be something he isn't.

Trying to be something you aren't is such a drag. What if you don't like making fun of people and threatening them and getting into trouble, like Garrett and Hubcap do? What if you like singing in Latin and making dragonfly lures and wearing a tie? Why can't you do what you want to do, be what you want to be?

Yeah, I like singing *"Dona Nobis Pacem."* I think it's cool to sing a song in an ancient language about peace. What's wrong with peace? I wish Garrett and Hubcap would leave me in peace. *Dona nobis pacem, dona nobis pacem.* I like peace.

I'm glad Mr. Weldon sent them to the office. Is that mean?

13. On Surviving Day One

On the way back to our class, the other kids start talking about Toulouse.

Monique: "Did you hear him sing?"

Ursula: "You call that singing? Mr. Weldon's right: he sounds like a bird."

Hubcap: "He's Mr. Weldon's new pet, that's for sure."

Garrett: "His pet weirdo, you mean."

Hubcap: "Yeah! His pet weirdo!"

Ursula: "I still want to know what happened to Otto."

Monique: "The way Toulouse stared at him was creepy."

She stops to squirt some hand sanitizer into one hand. She keeps a bottle of the stuff in her shoulder bag.

Ursula: "*So* creepy."

Garrett: "Totally. He's a freak."

Hubcap: "Totally."

Me: "Will you guys . . . why don't you . . . shut up?"

They all freeze. They don't expect this from me. Neither do I. It's one thing, though, when people say mean things about you. It's another when they say mean things about someone else. Especially someone nice like Toulouse. I can't imagine him saying mean things to anybody.

Before Garrett can get over his shock and shoot back an insult, Mr. Logwood comes over.

"Did I hear a disrespectful remark over here?" he asks.

"Yes, Mr. Logwood," Garrett says. "It was Woodrow. He told us to shut up."

I scowl at him. One of the rules at school—the *kid* rules—is that kids don't tell on other kids. If a kid does something against the adult rules, even if it's a kid you don't like, even if what he did is really bad, or even evil, it's against the rules to tell the adults.

The adults have to find out stuff on their own.

If I made the kid rules, I would get rid of this one. But I definitely don't make the rules. Kids like Garrett do.

However, another kid rule is that the kids who make the rules can break them whenever they feel like it. When you do as many mean things as Garrett does, you don't want other people telling on you. But he's allowed to tell, even on kids who didn't do anything wrong, even if he has to lie. He makes the rules, then he bends them or even breaks them whenever he feels like it.

"Woodrow?" Mr. Logwood asks, looking surprised. "Is this true?"

"They said . . . they were saying . . . mean things . . . about Toulouse."

This is the truth, but saying it is against the kid rules. No matter what I answered, I was in trouble here.

Garrett acts offended, but what he really is, is angry. He scowls at me. "That is not true, Mr. Logwood."

"Totally not true," Hubcap says.

Monique and Ursula look away. They're obeying the kid rules.

Mr. Logwood looks at all of us, one at a time. I can tell he believes me.

"Respect, students," he says. "Do I need to sing it?"

We all shake our heads. None of us want that.

14. Willow

I thought Toulouse would want to rush home after school. But he nodded when I invited him to go fishing, so we stopped at the office and called his house to get permission for him to get off at my stop. The secretary, Ms. Plowright, did the calling. She got the okay from Toulouse's mom, and he rode the bus home with me.

I guess this officially makes us friends. After telling Garrett to stop teasing him, I didn't really see any way around it. It was obvious to everybody that Toulouse and I were becoming friends. "Freaks of a feather flock together"— that's what Garrett said when Toulouse and I walked down the hall together to the office. I guess he's right.

My little sister, Willow, was a real pain on the ride home, pestering Toulouse with a billion questions.

"Why do you wear a suit like a grown-up?"

"Why do you wear a tie like one?"

"Why is your nose so pointy?"

"Why do you carry that instead of a backpack?"

"Where are you from?"

"Where do you live now?"

"Do you like it here?"

"Do you have a sister?"

"Why are you coming to our house?"

"Why do you keep staring at me like that?"

"Why won't you answer my questions?"

Mom's car wasn't in the driveway as my bus neared our stop. Usually she's home when Willow and I get there. Sometimes, though, she's still out on a job. My mom is a tree surgeon.

Dad's car is in the driveway. He's home, but he's probably sleeping, and we're supposed to be careful not to wake him. My dad works nights. He's a night watchman at a business park.

We go into the house and have a snack. I'm glad my mom isn't home. I want to show Toulouse around myself.

"We're going to my room," I tell Willow. "Do something quiet till Mom gets home. Dad's asleep."

"I *know*," she says with a scowl. "I'll play Librarian."

Librarian is a game she plays by herself. She checks books out to her stuffed animals, then she charges them fines when they don't return them on time. Like a stuffed animal could return a book.

Toulouse stands in the center of my room, holding his briefcase, looking as if he's waiting for me to say something, or maybe for a train in an old movie.

"Can I take your hat and coat?" I ask, just like Mr. Logwood did, only not as slowly.

Toulouse answers, "No, thank you."

He looks around at the stuff in my room, taking it in with his enormous eyes. He looks really interested, and suddenly I feel a little embarrassed. I haven't had a friend in here in a long, long time. Not since Farley Wopat, and that was in second grade. (Farley and his family moved away a few months later.) What does my room say about me?

It probably says I read a lot, but that I don't take such good care of my books. I rarely put them away. I stack them up like blocks and use them for stools, tables, and shelves. I leave them lying open, facedown, on the floor. I spill food and drink on them.

It probably also says that I like fiction, but that I read a lot of nonfiction, too. Books about fishing, rocketry, snakes, cryptids, weapons, raptors, semaphore, presidents, and lots of other things are mixed into the piles.

Visitors would also learn that I like duck tape. I keep a healthy supply of the stuff, in all sizes, colors, and patterns—including tie-dye, plaid, zebra, camo, mustache, penguin, zigzag, and candy corn—and I've created all sorts of things with it, including my lampshade, a few pillows, a couple of rugs, and a scratching post for our cats, Ouch and Meanie. Both cats were named by Willow, by the way, and both enjoy sharpening their claws on things made of duck tape. I made a duck tape scratching post hoping they'd leave my stuff alone. Instead, they leave the scratching post alone.

I guess my room also says I have cats. Cats who love duck tape.

"We have cats," I tell Toulouse, in case he's allergic. Lots of kids are.

He jumps.

"Don't worry," I say. "They're pretty harmless."

He starts trembling. Which makes me jittery. He looks nervously from side to side, by which I mean he swivels his head nervously from side to side. His shoulders don't budge.

"I m-mean, they hiss and swat, but they . . . they don't . . . you know . . . *injure* anybody or anything."

They do draw blood sometimes, but I don't tell Toulouse that.

"This is some stuff I found," I say, trying to change the subject. I walk over to my dresser, which is where I usually empty my pockets. I think of the pile as my midden, which is what a pack rat's stash is called. I'm proud of my stash, even if my parents and sister don't approve.

Toulouse approaches and looks it over carefully. Very carefully. He seems as interested in studying my jars of pebbles, glass shards, foil, wire, and other junk as he would be studying an encyclopedia, or an atlas, or a bowl of fish. In fact, he looks at it for so long that I start to wonder if we're going to do anything else this afternoon.

At least he's not freaked out about the cats anymore.

A knock on the door snaps him out of his trance. My mom steps in, wearing dirty brown work pants and a dirty denim work shirt. She's already taken off her tool belt, which is too bad. I'd like Toulouse to see her tools. My mom has good stuff.

15. Lynn

"Hey, Woodman," my mom says. Unlike Garrett's nickname, this is one I like, especially the "man" part. "Who's your little . . ." She stops when she sees how truly little Toulouse is. "Who's your friend?"

Mom knows enough not to interrogate Toulouse. She knows he and I are hanging out and to leave us alone. That's part of why she's such a great mom.

I tell her his name, and she says, "Nice meeting you, Toulouse. I'm Lynn. If you guys need anything, let me know," and leaves.

She wouldn't have gotten much info out of him anyway.

"Let's make some lures," I say.

He nods.

I like making lures. Flies, spinners, jigs—it doesn't matter. It feels good making things with my hands, including little things that require small motor skills and manual dexterity. We don't do things like that at school.

I get out my tackle box, which is an old steel lunch pail my dad found for me at a yard sale, and Toulouse takes his tackle box out of his briefcase. I have a vise attached to my drawing table for making lures, and, fortunately, I have a spare, so I attach it next to mine. Vises hold the lures securely while you work on them. Toulouse seems to know what I'm doing. I bet he has a vise at home. We get to work, stringing up some line, tying it off, then attaching things that will attract fish.

Certain fish like shiny things, and some like particular colors, or combinations of colors. Perch, in my experience, like purple, I've found. Croppies like feathers. Most of the fish I catch are sunfish, and they're not too fussy. They'll take about anything. After I catch them, though, I throw them back; they're too small.

When we've both made some lures, I go to

my closet to get a couple of rods. I have five or so, though I'm not sure where they all are. I give Toulouse the better one of the two. It has a reel that works. I also dig out two creels, which are little baskets to hold any fish we catch that are big enough to keep. Then we head out.

"We're going to the creek to fish," I tell my mom, who's stretched out on the couch with her laptop, studying a colorful table of words and numbers. Doing spreadsheets is part of a tree surgeon's job, too.

She checks her watch. "Okay, but don't be too long. It's getting dark earlier now." She looks at Toulouse. "Your parents picking you up or am I taking you home?"

"I will walk," he says in his hooty, breathy little voice.

He must like my mom to speak to her soon.

"Live nearby?" she asks.

I want to know this, too.

"Beyond the wood," he says. The last word goes on a while: "wooood."

I usually call it "the woods," but I like it without the s. It sounds fairy-taley.

Ouch saunters by and fires Toulouse a teeth-bared hiss.

Toulouse hops up onto a chair.

"Oh, Ouch," Willow says, waving him away. "Leave Toulouse alone. Sorry, Toulouse."

He gives her a nervous bow from the chair.

The cat hunkers off, his head low, glaring back at Toulouse.

"His parents know he's here, of course," Mom says to me, her eyebrows adding, *Right?*

"Uh-huh," I say.

"Then have fun. Catch me a whopper."

"Can I come with?" Willow asks. "I don't like to fish, but I can watch."

"No," I say.

She pouts. I look at Mom.

"We'll have fun here," she says to Willow.

"Want to play Librarian?" Willow asks.

"Sure," Mom answers, and smiles at me.

"Let's go," I say to Toulouse.

He hops down from the chair, gives my mom a bow, and we leave.

The wood (no *s*) is a few blocks away, past an open field. We don't live in town, but we don't live out of it, either. Kind of in between. We have neighbors, but their houses are far apart. Some of our neighbors have big gardens, or orchards, or fields with crops. One has a horse paddock. I often hear their horses whinny. I find lots of treasure for my midden in my neighborhood.

But today I'm not focusing on treasure. I'm focused on having company. Company *my age*, that is. Willow comes out with me sometimes, but that's different. She may be the same size as Toulouse, but she's not our age. I like having a friend over.

16. Out Here

When Toulouse and I enter the wood, the sun is low and shining at us like a giant motorcycle headlight through the trees. Mom's right: it is getting dark earlier.

Toulouse walks with his head tilted back, gazing up at the branches and the sky. He breathes in deeply and lets it out slowly. He's relaxed. I feel the same way.

It's quiet except for the sound of our feet snapping fir needles and the occasional tweeting bird. It's the opposite of school. No voices. No bells. No screaming or taunting or even whispering, except the wind through the branches. No teachers, no tests, no white-boards, no assignments, no walking single file. No Garrett. No Hubcap. Out here,

Toulouse and I aren't freaks. We fit in.

There aren't many bugs around the creek. It's too late in the year. Too cold. The water's high because it's been raining a lot. It's not roaring or anything—it's a small creek—but it's about as full as it ever gets.

Toulouse is good at casting. Casting isn't all that important on a creek this size, but it's fun to do, and I can tell he likes doing it. He gets a good swirl of line over his head, then, with a flick of his wrist, his hook, lure, and sinker shoot out over the water, then drop—*ploop!*

I stand upstream from him, giving him room, taking room for myself. A fisherman needs his own waters to fish. I make the first catch, a little sunfish, three or four inches long—too little to keep, too big for bait. I unhook it and throw it back. I glance over at Toulouse. He's staring at me as if he's shocked I threw the fish back.

He catches the next fish, and turns his body away as he unhooks it. I don't see him throw it back. I don't hear a *ploop!* I guess it must have been big enough to keep, and he tucked it into his creel.

I turn away and watch my line and listen to the creek gurgle. I read a biography of Isaac Newton once, partly because everybody had to read a biography for school, and partly because Isaac Newton happens to be one of my dad's heroes. The book said when Isaac was a kid he liked fooling around in creeks, and he grew up to be one of the most famous scientists ever. So there must be something good about fooling around in creeks, right?

Toulouse seems happy, too. He's a natural fisherman. Skillful. Calm. Patient. He's also a skillful, calm, patient painter, writer, and mathematician. How many kids do I know who would make the extra effort of not only writing with a quill and ink, but who would go to the bother of carrying that stuff around also? Not to mention an easel. And fishing tackle. Nobody I know.

Toulouse slips his hand into his coat and pulls out his pocket watch. He flips it open with a smooth motion, glances at it, then looks at me, frowning.

It's already time to head home.

We both sigh and start reeling in our lines. He finishes first and walks toward me.

"Where's your house from here?" I ask.

He points across the creek.

"How will you get across?"

Just then my hook snags the sleeve of my jacket. When I unhook it, it snags on my other sleeve. When I get it loose again and secure it to my reel, I look up and Toulouse is standing on the other side of the creek. He tips his hat, turns, and disappears into the trees.

I stand staring after him for quite a while, thinking. Then I notice that it's suddenly getting dark really quickly, so I start heading home.

Hoo! Hoo! a bird says in a flutish voice from somewhere.

I love the wood.

17. Weird Is Normal

"He's cute in his little suit," Willow says at dinner. "Hey, I rhymed! I'm a poet and don't know it!"

"Yes, you do," I say. "You just said you were."

She makes a sad face. "Oh."

"Toulouse is an artist, and he's also the smartest," I say.

"You're a poet and don't know it, too!"

"No, I know it."

"Wish I'd gotten the chance to meet him," Dad says.

Dad always wakes up in time for dinner. He'll leave for work at the business park after I'm asleep, and will be home and awake when I get up for school. It must be strange to be nocturnal.

Dad wears thick glasses with fragile-looking

wire frames. The frames are always bent, so his glasses always sit crooked on his face. Dad's balding on top and has a bushy mustache and adult braces on his teeth. He wears a tie without a jacket and a white, button-up, short-sleeved shirt. It's easy to imagine him as a science nerd when he was a kid.

Which he says he was. My dad loves science. He reads a lot of books about it, which is probably why I read so much nonfiction. He says he's always been a science nerd and often got teased about it when he was growing up. He also liked to stick things he found in his pockets. He still does.

He didn't become a scientist, though, because his family didn't have enough money to send him to college, and his grades weren't good enough to earn him scholarships. But he has always studied on his own. Being a night watchman gives him plenty of time to read. He calls himself an autodidact, a person who teaches himself, like Isaac Newton did. He says people probably used to call Isaac a science nerd, too—though, because he lived so long ago, probably not in those words.

"He was so little, Poppy," Willow says. "Littler than me!"

"That's not his fault," I say.

"No, if he could, I bet he'd be big like me. Everyone wants to be big."

Willow's pretty bubbly and talkative like this most of the time. It's cute, but sometimes it gets old.

"His hat was *adorable*!" she says.

"A bowler," Mom says to Dad.

"And he's from Quebec, eh?" Dad says. "Does he speak French or English? Or both?"

"He doesn't speak much at all," I say. "But he's spoken some French words and some English. And he seems to understand English pretty well. He had a French/English dictionary in his briefcase, and a quill and a bottle of ink, which is what he writes with. He loves fishing. And he makes lures. He keeps tackle in his briefcase, too."

"Sounds like your kind of kid," Mom says.

"The kids calls him weird. And odd."

"Weird *and* odd, eh?" Dad says with a laugh.

"And they made fun of him for being little."

"He *is* little," Willow says. "*So* little!"

That's what I mean about the cute stuff getting old.

"It's lucky he befriended you on his first day then, isn't it?" Mom says.

Mom is kind of weird, too, I guess, in her lumberjack clothes, and with her muscly arms and neck and her red, outdoorsy face. She never wears perfume or makeup, or girly clothes. She hates shopping, in fact. She loves rock and roll and blasts it when she's driving in her beat-up old truck. Not all moms play air guitar when they drive, I bet. Mine does.

She's normal to me, though. So is Dad. Even Willow, the bubbly librarian. Maybe weird is normal.

"I was thinking of inviting him over Saturday to fish some more," I say.

"I wonder if he wears the same clothes on the weekend," my mom says.

Dad shrugs.

"I bet he does," Willow adds.

So do I.

18. Loyalty

Toulouse didn't wear the same clothes to school the next day. Well, he wore the same jacket, gloves, and shoes, but today's black pants have gray pinstripes, the vest is dark red instead of black, his tie has a diamond pattern, and, on his head, he's wearing a brilliant red bowler.

Despite how beautiful it is, the hat gets laughs, which I doubt is why he chose to wear it. I wonder if he thought twice about wearing it, if he figured out that his wardrobe doesn't match ours, that the kids are teasing him because of it, but decided to go ahead and wear the red hat anyway, because he likes it.

That was my thinking back when I wore my duck tape clothes. But after months of being teased, I finally gave up. The fun of wearing them was spoiled by the snickering and taunting. I surrendered.

I wonder if Toulouse will. I wonder if he'll still be wearing a suit a month from now. I hope so.

"Good morning, Toulouse," I say as he unpacks his ink bottle and quill.

He tips his red hat. I wish I had one to tip back. It's so dignified, tipping hats. But they're not allowed in class.

"That was fun yesterday, at the creek."

He bows again.

"I was thinking we could go again, tomorrow, if you're free."

Tomorrow's Saturday.

"Are you guys dating?" Garrett interrupts.

Hubcap: "Yeah! You two going out?"

"We're *ten*," I say.

I glance at Toulouse, double-checking with my eyes. He nods. He's ten.

"So it's a *play*date," Garrett says.

Hubcap: "Yeah!"

"We're going fishing," I say, though I really

should ignore them. Like Toulouse does.

There's a beep, and the principal's voice comes out of the speaker. Saved by the morning announcements.

"Good morning, students. This is Principal McDowell. Please stand for the pledge."

We all stand and lay our hands on our hearts. Toulouse seems unsure about the hand-on-heart thing. Maybe they don't have to pledge allegiance in Quebec. He does lay his hand on his chest, but he doesn't recite the pledge with us. I doubt he knows the words. I don't even listen to what I'm saying when I say them.

"'. . . andtotherepublic . . . forwhichitstands . . .'"

The pledge ends. The principal introduces the two students who have been reading the announcements this month. I don't know them. William something and Olivia something. They're fifth graders.

"Photographers will be here today for Picture Make-Up Day," Olivia says, "for those of you who missed Picture Day in September."

And for those of us who lived in Quebec in September . . .

I glance at Toulouse. His eyes are opened very wide. They're as big as Oreos. He looks worried, bordering on scared. He must not like having his picture taken.

I know how he feels. "Smile," they say, but no one can. We grin instead. Grinning isn't smiling. When you grin you're either faking it or up to something.

I peek at Garrett. He grins at me. So does Hubcap.

Toulouse coughs. He coughs harder. He hacks. He's gagging on something.

I tap him on the back, swiftly but not hard. He keeps gagging.

"He's choking!" Ursula says. "During announcements! I can't *hear*!"

"Give him the Heimlich!" Monique says.

I stand up and wrap my arms around him, grip my left wrist with my right hand, and pull.

"*Hoof!*" Toulouse says.

Everyone shrieks. I hear something land on his desk. I'm behind him, so I can't see it.

Everyone sticks out their tongues in disgust. Whatever he coughed up is grossing them out. I step around.

The thing on his desk is about the size of a golf ball. It's dark brown, like dirt, and has fur. It's a dirt clod with fur.

And it came out of Toulouse.

19. Okay

I walk with Toulouse to the office, to see the nurse, as Mr. Logwood instructed. He also instructed me to ask that a janitor be sent to our classroom, and he instructed me to hurry — though we were not to run in the halls.

Before I left the room, I saw him use a paper towel to pick up the thing that Toulouse upchucked and seal it in a plastic sandwich bag. Maybe Mr. Logwood intends to have it analyzed. If so, I wouldn't mind seeing the results.

"I'm sorry you threw . . . you don't feel well," I whisper to Toulouse as we walk briskly down the halls.

He doesn't reply.

I'd like to ask what he ate for breakfast

this morning but decide it's too personal a question, and, most likely, rude.

"I am okay," he answers in a tiny voice.

"*Now*, you mean," I say. "I often feel better after . . . you know . . . after I vomit."

He nods.

At the nurse's station, I say, "Wait there . . . on that chair . . . for Edward . . . He'll take care of you. He's our nurse. I have to go talk to Ms. . . . the secretary."

"I am okay," he says again.

"Tell that to Edward . . . and don't worry . . . he's nice. He'll probably give you a mint for . . . for the taste. I'll see you back in the classroom. Edward will bring you there when he's done with you . . . after he's sure you're okay . . . which I'm sure you are."

"I am okay," he says for the third time.

"Right. So everything will be fine." I try to smile, which means I grin, then I walk away.

I tell Ms. Plowright that Mr. Logwood wants a janitor to come to our room to clean up a mess that a sick student made, and she picks up the phone.

In the hall on the way back, I think about how everyone will laser-beam poor Toulouse when he gets back to class. They'll melt his skin and bones and heart with their eyes. He'll be defenseless against them.

At least that's what it feels like to me after I do something stupid and get sent to the office. When I jammed the chopsticks down my throat, for example. And when I accidentally choked on a scented dry-erase marker. They make them smell too good.

I want to protect Toulouse, but how can I when I can't even protect myself?

I think about this as I walk through the halls, and come up with a plan that might work.

20. Works Like a Charm

I walk through the door. It's Read-Aloud. Mr. Logwood is sitting in his armchair in the Gathering Place, holding the book we've been reading, *Poppy*.

Hubcap, who can never focus during Read-Aloud, sees me first. He elbows Garrett, who swats at him. Garrett loves Read-Aloud. He gets completely absorbed in the stories and dislikes distractions to the point of hitting anyone who bothers him. When Hubcap elbows him again, Garrett shoots him a this-better-be-worth-it look. Hubcap makes a hitchhiker gesture toward me. Garrett glances over, and his face lights up. It's worth it.

Other kids sense that something is going on behind them and twist around. Within moments, I have the attention of the entire class. As planned.

On the way back from the office I stopped in the boys' bathroom and made a quick duck-tape bow tie and bowler. The hat is neon green. The bow tie is made of a duck tape with a mustache print. Those are the two tapes I happen to have in my pockets today.

The idea was that I'd attract the class's teasing away from Toulouse and onto me. And it's working like a charm.

"Is it Halloween already?" Garrett asks.

Hubcap: "Yeah, nice costume, Woody."

"That's enough," Mr. Logwood says, though he seems to be fighting snickers himself. "Or shall I break into song?"

Everyone shuts up.

"Maybe you'd like to hang up your hat, Woodrow," Mr. Logwood says to me.

"No, I'd like"—my throat closes up—"to keep it . . . on?" This last word I squeak.

"Like his *boy*friend," Hubcap says.

"Please take a Think Time, Vitus," Mr. Logwood says.

Hubcap stands and stomps away.

"Please, Woodrow," Mr. Logwood says. "As you know, wearing hats is not allowed in the building."

"You let Tou . . . Toulouse," I say.

"Yeah! If Toulouse can, why can't Woodrow?" Monique asks.

"It's only fair," Ursula says.

"Yeah!" Garrett says. Which surprises me— and everyone else. As a rule, Garrett does not stand up for me. Or anyone, except himself.

"Quiet, please," Mr. Logwood says. "This is Read-Aloud, which is intended as a quiet, listening time. If you do not wish to quietly listen, you can return to your desk and write a summary of the book so far."

Total silence, like someone hit the Mute button.

"Woodrow, I've been allowing Toulouse to wear his hat in class because he is new not only to this school, but to the United States, and I thought it best he be allowed to hold on to something that clearly gives him comfort during what must be a challenging transition.

In time, I'll ask him to comply with school rules. You, on the other hand, having attended Uwila since kindergarten, must certainly be used to our conventions and rules. I expect you to comply with them now."

He makes a good point. It's obvious from all the nodding that everyone agrees with it. I didn't think this all the way through. I got the attention I was after. I should have left it at that. I should have taken the hat off when he asked. Now my face is burning, and I feel as if I'm going to faint.

I remove my hat, then fumble with it, and end up dropping it. When I bend over to pick it up, stuff from my pockets spills out onto the floor with a clatter.

The snickering returns. I hope it lasts till Toulouse gets back, and he can slip in without notice.

21. Lenny the Magnet Boy

He doesn't return while I'm picking up my stuff.

He doesn't return during Read-Aloud.

He doesn't return by Writing Workshop, and I was hoping to do some peer editing with him on my story "Lenny the Magnet Boy," which is about a kid who gets magnetized after fooling around with his dad's metal detector. Forks and fish hooks and other metal stuff start flying at him. He ends up stuck to the refrigerator. I haven't come up with a decent ending yet, and I was hoping maybe Toulouse would have an idea.

Instead, I get paired up with Monique. It could be worse. It could be Ursula. Or Garrett.

Or Hubcap. Monique can actually be kind of nice. She says the story is funny, but she thinks some of the objects that fly at him would be too heavy. The hammers, for example.

"Good point," I say.

"But the hammers are funny," she says. "Maybe Lenny becomes a really, really strong magnet. Then he could attract something that he could use to pry himself off the fridge. Like a crowbar."

"Not bad," I say. "Not bad at all."

Monique's story is about a twelve-year-old girl named Natasha who finds out her mom and dad aren't her real parents, so she sets out to find them. She discovers they live in Paris and flies there to look for them.

"Alone?" I ask.

"Yes. She's very brave."

"But can kids . . . like . . . can they fly by themselves? I mean, don't you . . . don't they . . . have to have an adult . . . like a parent . . . with you . . . them?"

"My cousin flew here last summer by herself, and she's twelve."

"But I bet she had to have her parents' . . . Her parents probably had to fill out . . . you know . . . *forms*. And take her . . . to the airport."

She thinks about this.

"And Natasha . . . she's flying overseas," I say. "Wouldn't she . . . will she need a passport . . . or something?"

Monique thinks awhile longer, then says, "Maybe she finds out her parents live in the same town she lives in."

"Good idea, but not as exciting."

We start revising.

Toulouse isn't back by recess. I'm worried about him. Maybe Edward found something bad. Maybe Toulouse is very sick. I mean, who throws up things like that?

Music comes after recess on Fridays. Mr. Weldon teaches it. He does both music and choir, which makes sense.

Music class is different than choir, though. We don't sing. We play instruments. But not till after we've learned something about music. Today we learn about rests.

Some rests are one beat. Some are more.

Each one has a different symbol. They can be combined if the composer wants the musicians to pause for a length of time that doesn't have its own symbol. Six beats, for example, is a four-beat rest (called a whole rest) plus a two-beat rest (a half rest). Music is kind of like math, except you can hear it.

After we learn about rests, we practice, first by counting out loud as Mr. Weldon points at the written music on the overhead. Then we clap it. Finally, we get to use instruments. Everybody loves getting to use the instruments. Kids love making noise.

We usually don't get to use the instruments for long, though. Somebody always ends up banging on one of them too loud, or wielding one like a weapon, and then Mr. Weldon takes them away. It doesn't seem fair, especially with a kid like Hubcap in our class. A guy like him is always going to mess things up for everyone.

I like playing the castanets, which are tiny finger cymbals. If I were Lenny the magnet boy, I could suck them right to my hand. But I'm not, and I have to wait for my turn to choose an instrument. Unfortunately, Hubcap goes before me, and he knows I like the castanets, so he takes them. He doesn't even like them; he likes the loud instruments, the ones you bang, like drums and wood blocks. But I guess he likes messing with me more.

I take a recorder, and right after I do, Toulouse walks in. I'm so glad he's back that I run over to him.

"No running in class," Garrett says.

Hubcap shouts, "Yeah, Woody—walk!"

Mr. Weldon gives Hubcap a Think Time for shouting.

Nobody says a word about what happened before, when Toulouse choked. They're all too busy with their instruments. I guess in the end, I didn't need to make the duck-tape hat and tie. But I don't regret it. How can I? I still have the hat and tie.

22. Ooh-LOW

"Monsieur!" Mr. Weldon exclaims, and claps his hands together, his fingers pointed upward. *"Bienvenue,* Toulouse! Welcome! I worried you weren't going to be with us today! Here, for you, something special!"

He unlocks his off-limits supply cabinet with the small silver key he keeps on a chain around his neck.

"Come here, Monsieur Hulot!" He pronounces it *ooh-LOW*.

Toulouse walks over and looks inside.

"Take whichever instrument you like," Mr. Weldon says.

Toulouse looks up at him, then back into the cabinet. He leans in and comes out with a small red plastic accordion. It looks like a toy, but then all the instruments Mr. Weldon gives us look like toys. Toulouse pulls open the accordion, and it wheezes. The bellows are blue and made of cardboard. Toulouse covers some of the accordion's little buttons with his fingers and squeezes. It wheezes again, but this time there's a tune in it.

"Ah, you *play*!" Mr. Weldon says. "Please, monsieur, regale us with a song!"

I guess Toulouse doesn't have to count or clap first.

He pulls the accordion open again, and then squeezes it shut, then opens it again. He does know how to play it. He plays a song. It's cheerful, but with a slight sadness to it. Toulouse shuts his eyes and sways slightly. He plays an entire song, from memory.

Everyone is silent, then Mr. Weldon starts slapping his hands together loudly and cheering, *"Magnifique! Bravo! Bravo, Monsieur Hulot!"*

We start to clap and cheer, too. Some do so because they'll do anything if it means they get to make noise, but a lot of us mean it. We're impressed. I don't know if there's anyone in our class who can play a whole song on an instrument as well as Toulouse just did.

Toulouse bows twice.

When the clapping winds down, Mr. Weldon says, "That was 'Reine de Musette,' no?"

Toulouse nods.

"A beautiful tune, played beautifully!" Mr. Weldon gushes. He actually has tears in his eyes.

Then Garrett says in a loud voice, "What was that thing you puked up on your desk, Toulouse?"

"Yeah!" Hubcap says. "And what did you do to Otto?"

Mr. Weldon gets mad and sends them to the office.

I'm mad, too, and not just because they brought up the two things I didn't want brought up. I'm mad at Garrett and Hubcap because they hated the fact that Toulouse was impressing everyone and getting attention, so they decided to spoil it. They intentionally tried to embarrass him. It's mean to try to knock somebody down just because they're flying higher than you. Falling hurts more the higher you are. I know this from personal experience.

Toulouse puts the accordion back in the cabinet.

"Oh, please, monsieur," Mr. Weldon says, "won't you please play us another song?"

Toulouse picks up a triangle and comes over and stands next to me.

"Have it your way, monsieur," Mr. Weldon says, pouting.

I lean over and whisper to Toulouse, "I'd sure like to sock both of those guys right on their noses."

He looks up at me.

"'Sock' means 'punch,'" I say.

He nods.

"You're really good at the accordion."

He tips his hat.

"Okay, everyone," Mr. Weldon says. "Ready? All together now: One . . . two . . . three . . . ready . . . begin!"

We bang and shake and toot our instruments, making a pretty awful noise. We smile.

23. Winding and Unwinding

I'm a picky eater, and none of the few foods I like—pizza, chicken nuggets, nachos—are being served today. Lunch is beef stew, which smells weird and has green peppers, which I don't eat. The side dishes are not tater tots or french fries or even mashed potatoes, but steamed carrots and cole slaw. The dessert is red Jell-O. I may starve.

I fish out some beef chunks and slurp up the Jell-O, then dump my tray into the trash and head outside. Toulouse is up in his tree.

"How do you get up there?" I yell.

He stares at me a long time, then shrugs.

"I'll be right back."

I walk around, scanning the playground

for something to drag over and climb on, though I know there isn't anything. The adults have removed everything a kid could make something fun out of, or use as a weapon. All I find on the playground are kids, a recess teacher, some balls (which are, at the moment, being used by Garrett and Hubcap as weapons), and heavy play equipment sunk in concrete.

I turn around and trip over Toulouse.

"How do you do that?" I ask, helping him up and dusting him off.

He makes a hacking cough and a puff of dust comes out his mouth.

I'm relieved that it's only dust.

"You want to swing?" I ask. I see that two swings next to each other have opened up, a rare occurrence.

Toulouse picks up his briefcase, dusts it off, coughs again, then nods.

I take off running, yelling, "Dibs on the swings! Dibs on the swings! *Oof!*" I trip and fall on my face. And on a couple of rolls of duck tape, a compass, and my steel pencil sharpener, all of which are in my front pockets. Ouch.

No way will we get the swings now. I climb to my feet and look back at Toulouse.

He's not there.

I look at the swing set. There he is, perched on a swing, holding the chain of the one next to it.

"You can't save swings," Ursula says to him, her arms crossed angrily.

Toulouse stares at her.

I run over and dive at the swing. I land on it on my stomach. My momentum sends the swing back and up; it twists, then unwinds as it swings back down. I get dizzy, lose my balance, and fall off.

Ursula catches my swing and sits on it.

Toulouse hops off his and helps me up.

"Get out of the way!" Ursula yells at us.

Toulouse turns his head toward her and stares.

"Do it," she growls. "Move! Move now! Move, you little freak!"

"Respect," he says in his flutey voice.

24. Lion Eats Most of Boy

Toulouse shows me a story in another one of his old books. The book is called *Cautionary Tales for Children* and the story's title is "Jim, Who Ran Away from His Nurse and Was Eaten by a Lion"—which is a spoiler, if you ask me. The lion doesn't eat all of Jim. It doesn't get to his head, but only because the zookeeper comes along before it can. It doesn't seem fair to me that the lion eats Jim. All he did wrong was wander away from his nurse in a crowd. Getting eaten by a lion for wandering off seems harsh.

Strange that Toulouse showed me this story. Maybe he's a little angry at Ursula?

Next he shows me a story called "Godolphin Horne, Who Was Cursed with the Sin of Pride, and Became a Boot-Black." Godolphin is smug and rude. He doesn't shake hands and always smirks. He gets a chance to work as a page for the court, but, because he's so nasty, the king and a duchess and some bishops all say they don't want him. So Godolphin gets fired and becomes a poor shoeshine boy.

I think Toulouse is angry at Garrett, too.

When I finish it, I glance up at Toulouse and he has to cover his mouth to hide his laughter.

"Well, look at the worms," Garrett says from below us. We're sitting on the Ladder to Nowhere.

Hubcap: "Yeah, worms!"

"Worms?" Toulouse whispers to me. He seems scared. Or is he excited? It's hard to tell with his huge eyes.

"He means 'bookworms,'" I say. "It's what people who don't read call people who do."

It doesn't make sense that Garrett, who likes Read-Aloud so much, would make fun of reading. But then Garrett rarely makes sense.

"Who reads books on a playground?" Garrett asks, though it's not a question. He can see who does.

"Freaky bookworms!" Hubcap says.

"Worms," Toulouse says again, and licks his lips. He sure has a pointy mouth. It comes out at the center when he talks. Maybe it's because he grew up speaking French. People who speak French speak with real puckery lips. At least they do in movies. I haven't met anyone who speaks French except Toulouse and Mr. Weldon, and they both speak with puckery lips.

"What did you call us?" Garrett snarls.

Hubcap: "Did you just call us worms?"

"That's not . . . he didn't . . . ," I say.

"Why don't you come down here and say that?" Garrett says.

Hubcap: "Yeah!"

"He was . . . he just said . . . you know . . . he was *repeating* . . ."

"Just get down here, you chicken!" Garrett says.

Hubcap: "Bluck, bluck!"

"Chicken?" Toulouse says. Again, he licks his lips. Is he hungry?

"It's another expression," I whisper. "He's calling us scaredy-cats."

"*Cats?*"

This time he definitely looks scared.

"That's right, they're scaredy-cats," Garrett says, and elbows Hubcap.

Hubcap: "Yeah! Scaredy-cats! Meow, me—*Oof!*"

Toulouse lands on Hubcap's chest, knocking him flat on his back on the ground. Hubcap is stunned. Garrett is stunned. I'm stunned.

Toulouse stares deeply into Hubcap's wide eyes. Waiting for him—daring him?—to speak.

"I . . . I . . . I . . . ," Hubcap stammers.

"Not cats," Toulouse says to him, leaning in close. "No. *Cats.*"

I wait for Garrett to jump in and help Hubcap, but he doesn't. He just stands there with his mouth moving like he's talking, but nothing comes out.

It's nice to see both of them speechless for once.

The bell rings. Saved again. It's not a coincidence. Recesses are just really short.

Toulouse hops off Hubcap. Garrett rushes to his henchman and helps him to his feet.

"We'll take care of them later," he snarls.

Hubcap: "Yeah. Later."

They hurry away toward the building, glancing nervously back at us over their shoulders.

I'm still on the Ladder. I tuck Toulouse's book into his briefcase and click it shut. Suddenly, he's sitting next to me.

"Wow" is all I can think of to say.

He shakes his head. "No cats."

25. Our Zone

Toulouse enters a stall in the boy's locker room carrying a long gray duffel, then exits half a minute later wearing a baggy gray sweatsuit, black high-tops, and a red stocking cap. He's still wearing his gloves.

Garrett snickers and nudges Hubcap.

"Toulouse the athlete," Garrett says.

Hubcap: "Yeah!"

I'm tempted to point out how Toulouse just flattened Hubcap on the playground but decide to leave it alone. I'd probably just stutter anyway.

We're playing volleyball in P.E. this week. Ms. Otwell divides us into two teams. I volunteer to sit out the first game when it turns out the class is uneven. I pretend to be crushed as I walk toward the bleachers, but I don't mind at all. I avoid competitive sports whenever I can. I don't like them, and I'm clumsy, which gives Garrett and Hubcap more to taunt me about.

Toulouse follows me to the bleachers.

Everyone watches him. Garrett and Hubcap, of course, snicker.

"It's okay," I whisper to Toulouse. "Go on and play. Have fun."

He stays where he is.

Ms. Otwell comes over. "I have an idea, Woodrow. Why don't you and your new friend *share* a position."

How did she know Toulouse is my new friend?

"Yeah," Garrett says. "Put them together and you might make one whole player!"

Hubcap: "One who stinks!"

They both get warnings from Ms. Otwell. One more disrespectful outburst and they will sit out the game.

Toulouse and I take our position on the court, and the game begins. We're on the same team with Garrett and Hubcap, and they keep stepping in front of us to hit balls coming our way.

"Hit only the balls that come to your zone!" Ms. Otwell orders.

Garrett and Hubcap obey.

I don't know if volleyball is big in Quebec, but Toulouse seems pretty experienced at it. He easily returns the ball hit to us, though usually he sets up other players rather than hitting the ball back over. When someone sets him up, he leaps up and spikes. For such a little guy, he really gets off the ground. This could explain how he's able to get up and down from his tree and the Ladder and the swing set so fast, but it doesn't explain how he got across the creek. The creek is way too wide to jump across.

When our turn to serve comes, Toulouse aces it. Everyone stands there, gaping. Some people clap and cheer.

Is the kid good at everything?

Garrett and Hubcap aren't clapping or cheering. They are fuming. They have also noticed that I'm not exactly participating. I've been letting Toulouse hit all the balls that come to our zone.

"Hey, Woody!" Garrett says. "Can I get you a chair?"

Hubcap: "Yeah, Woody! Don't *do* something. Just *stand* there!"

Ms. Otwell gives them another warning. One more and they'll have to sit out the game.

Ms. Otwell doesn't always stick to her guns.

Toulouse holds the ball out to me. It sure looks huge in his hands. You can't even see his face.

"*You* serve, Toulouse," I say. "You're good at it. I'm not."

"Who?" he asks.

"Me! You serve."

He won't. He just keeps offering me the ball.

"I think Toulouse is saying it's your turn to serve, Woodrow," Ms. Otwell says.

Everyone starts getting restless and grumbling at me, so I take the ball. I toss it in the air, punch at it, miss, then it lands on my head. Everybody but Toulouse and Ms. Otwell crack up. Garrett laughs so hard I hope he chokes.

"Will you *please* serve?" I ask Toulouse.

He shakes his head. The kid's stubborn.

"Okay then," I say. "Get ready for strike two."

I toss the ball again, but this time I manage to hit it—into the back of Monique's head.

"Hey!" she screeches.

The gym echoes with laughter.

"Side out!" Ms. Otwell calls.

As we change positions, Garrett sticks his foot out and trips me. I don't fall all the way to the floor. I just squawk like a parrot because I think I'm going to.

Ms. Otwell finally follows through. "Take a seat on the bleachers, Garrett, and stay quiet or I'll send you to the office."

Garrett glares at me, then stomps over to the bleachers.

"Woodrow, take his zone," Ms. Otwell orders.

Hubcap glares at me as I obey.

I do the best I can during the game, which isn't great, but I do sometimes manage to hit a ball up in the air instead of miss it, or punch it into the net, or into the ground, or into one of my teammates' heads.

Toulouse gives me encouraging smiles and nods whenever I look over at him. When I do particularly well, he claps.

I'm sort of enjoying myself.

In P.E.

Now that's weird.

26. Wink

People are different toward Toulouse after the game. Interested. Attentive. All because he was good at volleyball. That's what happens when you excel at competitive sports. Before that he was the weird freak in the weird clothes who maybe swallowed, then regurgitated our fish and definitely coughed up a furry golf ball. Now, he's fascinating. A star.

He's not crazy about it. After the game, he hides behind me as best he can. Then he disappears. A couple of minutes later, he walks out of the locker room, fully dressed.

When we're back in class, Monique comes up to me.

"Woodrow, can you make duck-tape bangles?"

"What?" I ask. I'm not sure she's talking to me. She doesn't usually ask me things out of the blue. Also, I'm not sure I know what bangles are.

"Can you make me some bangles out of duck tape." She shakes her arm, and her bracelets clink together.

"Oh, *bangles*," I say. "Sure . . . I guess . . . but they wouldn't . . . I don't think they would . . . duck tape doesn't . . . well . . . *clink*."

"Good point," she says seriously, and shakes her bangles again. "I need them to clink."

"Come on, Woody, can't you make them clink for her?" Garrett asks. "What kind of girl's-jewelry maker are you?"

Hubcap snickers.

I ignore him.

"They won't clink, but I could make . . . if you want one . . . I could make a . . . what do you call it? . . . A . . . one of those princessy crown things . . . if you . . . you know . . . want . . ."

She shakes her head. "I don't want a tiara."

"Right—a tiara. No, okay . . . how about a little purse thing? . . . maybe a wallet?" I pull out my duck-tape stash. "Like, a small bag with a flap . . . maybe Velcro? . . . for your hand sanitiz—"

I don't finish because I'm not sure I should be mentioning her hand sanitizer. She always has some with her, and it's never in the same bottle, like she has a collection. I'm not sure what it's all about, but I'm not judging. I'm sure she wonders about me and my duck tape. I know she does. She's made fun of me about it before. I don't want to make fun of her.

Monique has collected a lot of different things over the years. She used to love erasers, the kind you stick on the ends of pencils. She had a million of them. Then one day, no more erasers. Instead, she loved stickers. She stuck stickers on everything. Then, gone. Next it was buttons, the kind with pins on the back and sayings on the front, like YOU SAY POTATO, I SAY TATER TOT and I'M CORRECTING YOUR GRAMMAR IN MY MIND. Her jackets and her backpack were covered with them. Now it's bangles.

"Yeah," she says dreamily. "A clutch purse. I like clutches."

Maybe clutches will be her next thing. Maybe duck-tape clutches.

"Why don't you draw . . . you're a good . . . draw a picture of . . . you know . . . what you want? . . . And write down the colors you want . . . where you want them . . . and I'll . . . I can make it . . . easy."

"Well"—she says, ripping a piece of paper out of her notebook—"it should be a rectangle, of course . . ." And she draws one, then adds a triangular flap.

"Okay," I say. "I could make a hole? . . . For you to close it?" I draw a line across the flap. "It could . . . you know . . . tuck in. . . ."

She nods, and draws a second line. "Two slits. It could go in one and out the other. That would hold better."

"Good idea," I say. "Very . . . clever." My face feels hot.

"Thanks," she says.

"I can . . . I'll make it . . . as soon as I can."

"Okay, gang, let's line up," Mr. Logwood says. "A good day. Well done."

We line up to leave. I'm behind Ursula and

Toulouse. Toulouse turns his head all the way around and winks at me.

I wonder why.

Did he have something to do with Monique's request?

Maybe he's just letting me know he noticed that Monique was nice to me. Does he understand already how unusual that is?

Maybe the wink had nothing to with Monique. Maybe it was just a friendly wink. When it comes to people acting friendly toward me, I'm not the best judge. I'm a little rusty.

Maybe I'm overthinking this. I have a tendency to do that.

Maybe it was just a wink.

I wink back.

27. Little Weirdo

While we're waiting in line to leave, I overhear Garrett talking to Hubcap.

Garrett: "So the little freak can hit a volleyball. Big deal."

Hubcap: "Big deal."

Garrett: "I can hit a volleyball better than he can, but the teacher wouldn't let me play."

Hubcap: "Right. So unfair."

Garrett: "He's still a little weirdo."

Hubcap: "So weird."

Garrett: "A freak."

Hubcap: "Exactly. A weird little freak."

I look for Mr. Logwood, hope he's hearing this, but he's across the room at his desk, stapling together papers, probably for us to take home.

"Watch this," Garrett says.

Hubcap: "What are you going to do?"

"Just watch."

He walks up to Toulouse and me.

"Hey, Toulouse," he says. "Your shoe's untied."

Is he kidding? That's the oldest trick in the book. But before I can warn him, Toulouse tilts his head forward to look at his shoes, which, of course, are tied. Garrett quickly slaps the brim of Toulouse's red bowler and it sails up into the air.

While everyone else watches the hat twirling overhead, I watch Toulouse scoot under the nearest desk. He doesn't even have to duck. He peers out with terrified eyes.

I spring up and snatch the hat out of the air. I smoothly feed it to Toulouse under the desk, then turn to face Garrett. If blood boils, that's what mine is doing. Garrett has done a lot of mean things to me over the years, but I don't think any of them ever made me this mad.

"You . . . ," I say. That's the only word that comes out.

He covers his mouth and snickers. So does Hubcap. This makes me even madder.

"You . . . are . . ." Oh, dear. Is this going to come out one word at a time?

More snickering. Toulouse steps out from his hiding place, the hat back on his head, and stands beside me. This gives me courage. And purpose.

"Cruel," I finish. "You are cruel. From now on . . . from now *on* . . ."

I know what I want to say, but suddenly I'm aware everyone is listening, and the words get literally stuck in my throat. I can feel them down there, hiding like Toulouse under the desk, afraid to come out. Finally, my anger pushes them free.

"Leave . . . Toulouse . . . alone," I say. This time I'm not stammering. I'm speaking slowly and clearly, so that he can't misunderstand me. "And while you're at it, leave *me* alone, too."

"Yeah," Monique says. "Stop being a bully, Garrett."

"What'd I do?" he asks.

"You knocked his hat off," I say. "And you and Hubcap went through his briefcase. And you tried to trip me in gym." Boy, I'm on a roll. "And you called Toulouse names. Mean names. Like you call me. 'Freak.' 'Dork.' 'Worm.' And you tease us just because we're friends."

"Friends," Toulouse says.

"Right," I say, peeking down at him.

Hubcap snickers.

"You do it, too," I say to him. "You do every mean thing Garrett does, you little copycat."

"Cat?" Toulouse says.

"No," I whisper to him. "No cat."

Mr. Logwood finally comes over, and people back up to let him through.

"Everything okay over here?" he asks, looking at Garrett and Hubcap, then at Toulouse and me. "Woodrow? What's happening?"

I can't speak. I have a lot to say, but the words rush to my throat so fast they create a traffic jam.

"My shoes are tied, Garrett," Toulouse says.

Garrett can't help himself. He snickers. Hubcap, too.

"Garrett knocked Toulouse's hat off," I say. "And he called him names. Mean names. He's been doing it a lot."

"Is that true, Toulouse?" Mr. Logwood asks.

Toulouse's head pivots to Garrett. He blinks. I see those diagonal lines again. He pivots to Hubcap. He blinks. He's telling on them without telling.

"It *is* true, Mr. Logwood," Monique says.

Ursula nods. A lot of kids nod. I'm not the only one who's tired of Garrett's and Hubcap's meanness.

"What is a 'weirdo'?" Toulouse asks Mr. Logwood.

"All right, Garrett, Vitus, please go over to the Gathering Place," Mr. Logwood says. "I'll meet you there in a second."

They hang their heads, but before they walk away, they flash Toulouse and me spiteful looks. This isn't over.

"I'm sorry, Toulouse," Mr. Logwood says. "Please trust that the boys' behavior will not be tolerated."

Toulouse bows.

Mr. Logwood smiles, bows back, then walks away.

Toulouse reaches up and sets his gloved hand on my shoulder. *"Merci,"* he says, staring into my eyes for an uncomfortably long time.

"Sure," I say to break the trance.

It doesn't work.

By the time Mr. Logwood's talk with Garrett and Hubcap ends, the school day is over.

"We have to stay in for recess all next week because of you two little freaks," Garrett whispers menacingly when he returns.

Hubcap: "Yeah."

"You are *so* going to get it, Woody," Garrett says.

This is how they act after getting punished for being mean? Then again, what did I expect, sudden transformation?

The funny thing is that their threats don't bother me. Things have changed. Toulouse is my friend now, and somehow that makes me feel stronger, more comfortable in my oddness. It's harder to feel like a weirdo when there's someone who's as weird as you are. And it's harder for Garrett and Hubcap to scare me when I'm not facing them alone. And it isn't just Toulouse and me facing them. Lots of kids, including Monique and Ursula, stood up for us. And I bet Mr. Logwood will be doing more about the way they treat us than singing a little song.

But mostly things are different because I'm different. I feel braver. Stronger. I'm not going to let Garrett push me around, or put me down, anymore.

"When are we going to get it?" I ask Garrett. Again, I'm not stammering. "At recess?"

"No recess," Toulouse chirps.

Garrett's eyes flash with anger. Hubcap's, too.

I put my arm around Toulouse's very low shoulders. "Oh, that's right. You guys have to stay in during recess. All next week."

I grin.

28. Only Friend

"What are you making?" Willow asks me.

"You didn't knock," I answer.

"Sorry, what are you making?"

"You're supposed to knock before you come in."

"Do you want me to knock now?"

"It's a clutch."

"What's a clutch?"

"It's like a purse, only you hold it in your hand."

"No strap?"

"No strap."

"What's the point of a purse if it doesn't have a strap?"

"I don't know. It's not for me."

"Who's it for?"

"A girl at school. She asked me to make her one out of duck tape."

She pauses to think, then asks, "Will you make me one?"

"Sure."

"Do you still have the candy-corn duck tape?"

"Yup."

"I'd like mine made of that, please."

"After I finish this one."

"Who's the girl? Is she a friend of yours?"

"Her name is Monique."

"Isn't she the one you like?"

"She's okay."

"Was Toulouse at school today?"

"Yes."

"Was he nice to you?"

"Yes."

"Why don't you make him a clutch?"

"I don't think he'd want a clutch. He's a boy."

"Well, make him something he does want then."

I pause to think. If anyone deserves a

present from me, it's Toulouse. What would he like? Duck tape isn't really his style.

"You could make him a hat. He likes hats."

True, but his hats are so old-fashioned.

"I'll think of something," I say.

"Do the kids still make fun of him?" Willow asks.

"Not really. I think they're starting to appreciate him. They saw how good he is at painting, and at playing the accordion, and at hitting a volleyball."

"A volleyball?"

"Yeah. Garrett and Hubcap weren't impressed, of course. They kept on being mean to him. They called him names. They even got into his personal stuff."

"Oh!" she says, steamed. "Big bullies!"

Willow is very protective about her personal stuff.

"Exactly. Finally, Garrett knocked Toulouse's hat off, and I told him he was cruel and he needed to leave Toulouse alone. I had to protect Toulouse, you know?"

She nods seriously.

"Monique said Garrett was being mean, too."

"That's the girl you're making a clutch for?"

"Uh-huh."

"Does she like Toulouse?"

"I think she does. Then Mr. Logwood had a talk with Garrett and Hubcap, and they have to stay in for recess all next week."

"They deserve it!"

This makes me smile. I like how she stands up to injustice. I think she'll be better at it than I am.

"So everything's all right now?" she asks.

"Sure," I say, and laugh. Little kids can be so naive.

"And Toulouse is your best friend now?"

"He's really my only friend."

"No. I'm your friend, Woodman."

"Thanks, but that doesn't really count."

"Of course it *counts*."

She picks up a roll of duck tape with a pink zebra pattern.

"Can I make something, too?"

"What do you want to make?"

The last time I let her make something out of my duck tape, she ended up making a big wad of duck tape, then just walked away.

"I don't know," she says. "Maybe a purse? You know, with a handle? I could make the handle with the penguin duck tape."

"I don't have much left after your last project."

"See? We *are* friends. You're letting me have all your penguin duck tape."

"Maybe. Get a chair and I'll teach you how to make a purse, so you won't use up all of my pink zebra, too."

29. Wood

Toulouse lives in a tree house. A *tree* house. It's a house built into a *tree*.

His whole family lives in it, of course. The wood it's made out of still has the bark on it, which helps to camouflage the house—if that's what they were thinking when they built it. Most people's homes aren't camouflaged. I wish ours was. Theirs is so cool. I bet it's even harder to see when the trees aren't bare. In the spring, with the leaves, it must blend right into the wood.

The house isn't even on a paved road. They built it deep in the forest, away from everything, and everyone. There's no lawn or sidewalks or driveway. If they own cars, I don't see them. There are a couple of bicycles leaning against a neighboring tree. One of them has a covered trailer attached to it.

Toulouse meets me outside the house. He's wearing his suit and hat. He doesn't have his briefcase.

"Welcome," he says with a bow.

"Thanks," I say, and automatically bow back. I'm getting into the habit.

Following him, I climb the wooden spiral staircase that winds around the house's trunk, up to the front door. The knob is made of wood. Toulouse turns it and pushes open the door.

In the entryway, there's a wooden hat rack that looks like a tree. Its branches are the hooks, and the hooks are overflowing with hats. Toulouse starts to take off his hat, but then abruptly twists his head toward me, as if he forgot he had a guest. He ushers me into the next room, leaving the hat on his head.

I wonder why he changed his mind like that. Why doesn't he ever take it off? Is he hiding something under it? Is that why he hid under the desk when Garrett knocked his hat off?

We walk through a low archway into the

kitchen, which has a low, domed ceiling. His mom stands at the stove, wearing a long dress and old-fashioned lace-up boots. She's also wearing a pale pink bonnet with a ribbon that ties under her chin. It all seems a bit fancy for the kitchen.

She turns her head toward us without turning her body, like Toulouse does. She has large eyes, too, larger than Toulouse's, but then she's bigger than he is. She's not very tall, though. I think she's shorter than I am. She wears little granny glasses perched on her nose, which is as pointy as Toulouse's.

"Hello, Woodrow," she says, and curtsies. Her voice is deeper than Toulouse's, but just as flutey. Oboey, maybe. We studied the woodwind family last month in Mr. Weldon's class.

"Hello," I say. I don't want to call her Ms. Hulot in case I pronounce it wrong. Also, for some reason, "Ms." doesn't suit her. She seems too old-school for it. She's more like a "Mrs." Or, since she speaks French, maybe "Madame"?

She smiles and stares at me. I try to think of something to say. I laugh uncomfortably.

She looks at Toulouse.

"Come," he says, tapping my shoulder.

As we leave the kitchen, I look back at his mom. She's dropping something into the tall, steaming pot on the stove. It's small and gray with . . . fur?

Toulouse pulls me away and leads me up another spiral staircase, this one inside the house. On the next floor, which has ceilings so low I have to stoop over, we pass what must be his parents' bedroom. It's dark in the bedroom, and there appears to be someone in the bed, snoring. Toulouse presses a gloved finger to his pointy lips. He's telling me to be quiet.

"Papa works nights," Toulouse whispers.

"Mine, too," I say.

Toulouse's bedroom has a loft. He has to climb a ladder made of logs sawed in half lengthwise to reach his bed. No wonder he's so good at jumping: his house has a million steps. He has to literally climb into bed.

The next thing I notice about his room are his collections. He keeps things in old glass bottles and cases: bird nests, dead insects, pebbles, feathers of all sizes, bottle caps, rusty nails and screws, pull tabs, fish hooks . . . He also has a collection of small square bottles, empty but stained with ink, on his windowsill. He has several wooden fishing poles. They look hand-carved. There's an easel in the corner with a canvas on it. He's in the middle of painting a picture of the creek. It looks realer than the real thing.

I love his room. It reminds me of mine.

He picks up a rod and an old, sturdy tackle box. He gestures for me to follow.

We tiptoe by his snoozing dad, back down the spiral staircase. We stop in the kitchen.

"*Salut!*" he says to his mother, with a tip of his hat.

She says something in French in return.

He nods.

It must be fun to speak to your mom in another language.

30. Lunch

We walk through the wood toward the creek. It's Saturday morning, so we can take our time. We don't talk. We look at the trees and listen to the birds and our feet snapping the fir needles. The forest has a high ceiling, like the gym, or a theater. It's big and airy and still. It would be hard to climb these trees. The lowest branches are pointy stubs, way above our heads. The real branches are very high, reaching for sunlight.

At the creek, Toulouse and I sit side by side on a big log and open our tackle boxes. I show him some flies I made with duck tape.

"This one I made for you," I say. Making him a gift was Willow's idea, of course, but I don't mention that.

He takes it with a little bow and a *"Merci."*

"Why don't you try it out?" I ask.

He nods, then walks away to find his own waters.

I'm not wearing a watch. If Toulouse has his pocket watch, he doesn't check it, and I don't ask him to. Who cares what time it is? It's Saturday.

The sun keeps creeping across the sky, creating a slowly moving web of shadows over us and the creek. The morning goes by without bells or schedules, without standing in lines. It's Think Time all the time. Or maybe Not-Think Time. It's Silent Sustained Fishing.

My stomach tells me when it's lunch, not a clock or a bell or Mr. Logwood's schedule on the whiteboard. Toulouse and I return to the big log.

"Did you catch anything big enough to keep?" I ask. It's the first sentence I've said in a while, and it comes out gravelly.

I saw him catch quite a few fish. They all looked pretty small. I didn't notice him throwing any back.

He opens his wicker creel to show me it's empty.

"Toulouse?" I ask.

He looks up at me.

"Can I ask you a question?"

It's the Otto thing. I haven't been able to get it out of my mind.

"Did you . . . ? And then . . ."

I can't ask. I don't want him to think I'm accusing him of anything.

"Never mind," I say.

He nods, but keeps looking at me. Staring at me, really. It's like he wants me to ask him something.

I certainly have plenty of questions for him. There's a lot of things I don't understand. Like the furry golf ball he coughed up. And the way he appears and disappears so quickly. And the dropping out of trees without getting hurt. And the getting up them in the first place. And crossing the creek. There's also the way he turns his head around backward. And those weird diagonal lines in those huge, round eyes of his. Nobody's eyes are that big.

And his nose. Nobody's nose is that sharp. And, of course, there's the never taking off his hat, or gloves. I've never seen the top of his head, his hair, or his hands. Does he wear so many clothes because he likes to, or because he's hiding something?

And why didn't he want his picture taken? What was he afraid of? Is he a vampire or something?

He keeps staring me as I think about all of this, then at last he asks, "Food?"

He lifts the upper level of his tackle box and, from beneath it, takes out a sandwich wrapped neatly in wax paper.

I let go of my questions, and say, "Sure."

I brought along lunch, too: a PBJ and nacho-flavored tortilla chips. We unwrap our sandwiches and, at the same time, bring them up to our mouths. A tiny pink foot is dangling from his.

Toulouse senses me looking at the foot. He gives me the same look he did when he almost took off his hat.

And my mind starts putting things together,

coming up with answers to my many questions, answers that make sense but are completely, and insanely, impossible.

I set my sandwich on my lap.

"T-Toulouse?" I ask. "Are you . . . I mean . . ."

He tilts his head, listening.

"You're not an . . ."

I can't finish the sentence. It's too crazy. Of course he isn't. He can't be. He wears clothes. He goes to school. He reads. He paints. He plays the accordion. He can't be an . . .

But then again, it is all so *odd* . . .

"Woodrow?" he asks. "You okay?"

So *weird* . . .

"Woodrow?"

He inches over toward me. His legs don't reach the ground. He is so *little*.

Odd. Weird. Little.

O . . . W . . .

"Want some?" he asks, holding out his sandwich. The pink foot swings.

"I'm good," I say.

He's leaning in very close to me now. He blinks, and I see the diagonal lines again, one in each enormous eye. This is the closest I've ever gotten to him. His skin is fuzzy. No, not fuzzy. Not furry, either.

Feathery?

He smiles, nods, and tips his hat. All the way off his head.

And I see what he is.

31. Odd, Weird, and Little

I was right. What he is, is impossible. And crazy. And incredible. I suppose this is why I never saw it. Why no one did. Not even the adults: the teachers, the principal, not even Mom. If they did see it, they would have convinced themselves they didn't. It's too crazy. Too impossible. But if we had looked at Toulouse, really *looked* at him—past the weird grandpa suit and hat, the briefcase filled with so many odd things, his littleness and foreignness—we would have had to admit what he was.

And anyone who looked at him closely would feel what I'm feeling right now. Frightened. Shocked. Confused. As if suddenly all the rules we'd made up about the world were wrong. As if your own eyes couldn't be trusted. As if some weird dream you never had had came true. As if you had lost your mind.

I'm feeling and thinking all of these things at the same time. They are crashing down on me. I feel as if my brain is being wrung out like a rag, my heart is blowing up like a balloon, my legs have turned to rubber. Seeing how Toulouse is something that just can't be is changing me. I'm pretty sure I'm going to faint. Yep, here I go. . . .

"You okay?" Toulouse asks, bracing my arm with his gloved hand.

I jerk awake. I look at him. I really look at him.

And it's okay. I'm okay. More than okay. I feel proud. Proud that Toulouse showed me who he is. Proud that I was the first to see him. Proud to be his friend. I hope I am for a long time.

This will depend on who else discovers what he is. Imagine if Garrett found out!

No. No one must find out.

One thing's for sure. No one will ever find out from me.

"I'm okay," I say to Toulouse.

"Good," he says.

He dives into his sandwich. He doesn't chew. He swallows his food whole, pink foot and all.

Patrick Jennings

is the author of many popular novels for middle-schoolers, including *Guinea Dog*, *Lucky Cap*, *Invasion of the Dognappers*, *Guinea Dog 2*, and *Faith and the Electric Dogs*. *Guinea Dog* won the 2013 Kansas William Allen White Children's Book Award, the 2011 Washington State Scandiuzzi Children's Book Award, and received an honor in the 2013 Massachusetts Children's Book Award. That novel also appeared on the following state lists: the 2011 Colorado Children's Book Award, the 2010-2011 New Hampshire Great Stone Face Book Award, the 2012-2013 Florida Sunshine State Young Reader's Award, the 2014 Washington State Sasquatch Award, the 2014 Hawaii Nēnē Award, and the 2014-2015 Indiana Young Hoosier Book Award. He lives in a small seaport town in Washington State.

You can visit him online at www.patrickjennings.com.

Sellj

JERRY

ON THE LINE

by Brenda Seabrooke

BRADBURY PRESS
New York

Collier Macmillan Canada
Toronto
Maxwell Macmillan International Publishing Group
New York   Oxford   Singapore   Sydney

Bradbury Press
An Affiliate of Macmillan, Inc.
866 Third Avenue, New York, NY 10022

Collier Macmillan Canada, Inc.
1200 Eglinton Avenue East
Suite 200
Don Mills, Ontario M3C 3N1

Printed and bound in the United States of America
First Edition
10 9 8 7 6 5 4 3 2 1

The text of this book is set in 12 point Baskerville.
Book design by Julie Quan

Library of Congress Cataloging-in-Publication Data
Seabrooke, Brenda.
    Jerry on the line / by Brenda Seabrooke. — 1st ed.
        p.   cm.
    Summary: Fourth grader Jerry, latchkey kid and aspiring soccer star, starts an unusual friendship with a younger latchkey kid when she calls his number by accident.
    ISBN 0-02-781432-7
    [1. Latchkey children—Fiction.   2. Soccer—Fiction.
3. Friendship—Fiction.]   I. Title.   PZ7.S4376Je   1990
[Fic]—dc20 90-1745   CIP   AC

To my son Kevin—a once, present, and always hero

CHAPTER 1

"Beat'cha to the playground," Ricky said.

"Oh, yeah?" Jerry yelled over his shoulder as he jumped off the last two steps of Van Vickle Elementary. "This is gonna be a soccer day."

"You better get going then," Joel said. He was Jerry's best friend and always on his side. "Beat Tank."

Jerry was already running. He spotted a Pepsi can in the alley ahead and sped toward it. He gave it a mighty thwack with his foot. The can spun through the air. Jerry raced after it.

He could almost hear the announcer's voice.

1

"The first kick of the afternoon by the fabulous JJ Johnson, soccer fans, and it is a beaut!"

Jerry liked to run after being cooped up in the fourth grade all day. It felt good to limber up and stretch his legs. Also, practicing with the can was good for his soccer game. Jerry lived for soccer. He wanted to be a soccer star when he grew up. Everybody knew that sport stars were heroes. He planned to be a soccer star and a hero, too, and he needed all the soccer practice he could get.

Jerry had another reason for racing through the alleys. He had to get home in a hurry. Before he could go to the playground every day, he had to go home and check in with his mother by phone. It was a rule. So instead of walking with his friends, he took a shortcut. He could get home sooner running through the alleys. Then he could get to the playground faster, before Tank or any of Tank's friends. The unwritten rule of the playground was that the first kid there got to choose the game for the day. Jerry wanted to be first so he could choose soccer. The spring soccer season was only a few months away, and he wouldn't be able to practice after the snow fell.

The can skimmed ahead of Jerry. He caught up to it and kicked it hard, straight up the middle of the alley. A real bomb. A bullet. If he'd been on the soccer field, he bet it would have gone right between the goalie's legs.

Jerry reached the last alley. He tried to cover it with one kick. He let his momentum carry him as he came up on the can. Without breaking stride, he swung his left foot. *Whambo!* The can shot forward with Jerry right behind.

He was going to make it. The can hit the ground halfway down the alley but that was okay. It would roll the rest of the way unless something blocked it, something like that old bicycle tire right in the can's path. Jerry put on a burst of speed. He reached the tire an instant before the can did and whipped the tire out of the way. The can rolled by.

Saved in the nick of time by Jerry Johnson. The crowd went wild. The announcers gave up trying to be heard as the crowd roared, "JJ! JJ! JJ!"

The can rolled to a stop at the edge of the sidewalk. Jerry crossed the street and went in the door of his apartment building. He was almost two blocks ahead of his friends from school. Ricky and Abe were probably in the lead but that was okay. He knew he could beat them to the playground. It was Tank he really had to beat. Tank

3

always chose football. But even Tank had to go home first.

Jerry needed to play soccer. He had to play soccer. He sprinted up the stairway to his floor and down the hall. He counted off the doors. Almost there. He skidded to a stop in front of his door. He could hear the telephone ringing inside.

CHAPTER 2

Jerry pulled out his door key. He loved coming home by himself and unlocking the door with his own key. He could hear the phone inside still ringing.

"I'm coming," he yelled through the door. But just as he slid the key into the lock, the ringing stopped. Jerry wondered who had called. His mother wouldn't call this early.

Jerry liked being a latchkey kid. He was glad his parents trusted him with his own key. They were saving to buy a house and maybe a trucking rig for his father. His mother had gone back to work last summer so they could hurry things along. They were able to save even more because they didn't have to pay for a sitter for Jerry.

Jerry would never forget the day his parents had given him his key. They'd made it into a celebration. His dad had brought home Chinese carryout and a chocolate cake from the bakery for dessert. Then they had given him a box wrapped in shiny silver paper tied with a silver ribbon. Inside, on a bed of cotton, had been a key to their apartment door. It was on a chain. As Jerry had proudly hung it around his neck, his dad had said, "Now you can help us save for the new house."

Most of Jerry's friends were latchkey kids, too. Only David's mother stayed at home, but he had a new baby brother. David always told people he would be a latchkey kid soon.

Jerry slipped the chain over his head and stuffed the key back under his shirt. Scooter and John wore their keys on their belts with a bunch of other old keys they'd found in a trash dump. Their keys jangled when they walked and made them feel important. Jerry didn't want to carry more than one key. The weight would slow him down.

Sometimes at school he wore the key outside

his shirt to impress a new kid or a teacher. A latchkey kid was somebody special, Jerry thought, somebody who knew how to take care of himself.

Jerry liked coming home to an empty apartment. He pretended he was grown up and coming home from his job to his own place where nobody could see anything he did. He could put his feet on the coffee table in front of the sofa and drink his milk without anybody to see his milk moustache and tell him to use a napkin. Or he could lick the plate his cake had been on and nobody was there to tell him to mind his manners.

But there were rules. His parents were very strict about the rules. They were posted on the door of the refrigerator, held up by the four magnets shaped like soccer balls that he had given his mother for Christmas to hold recipes and things.

1- Walk straight home from school.
2- Don't bring anybody home with you.
3- Don't open the door for anybody.
4- Keep the door locked at all times.
5- Wait for Mom's call.
6- Don't call her office except in an emergency.

Jerry's mother called every day at the same time to see that he had gotten home safely. She was a receptionist at a clinic. He wasn't supposed to call her there because personal calls were only for emergencies. So far there hadn't been an emergency. When his dad was home the rules didn't apply, because then Jerry wasn't a latchkey kid, although he was allowed to keep his key. But his dad was a trucker and away a lot.

Jerry made a quick sandwich while he waited for his mother's call. He mashed up a banana with peanut butter and spread it on two slices of bread. The banana was mushy, the way he liked it because when he mixed it with crunchy peanut butter, the gooey goop spread more easily. He took a big bite and poured a glass of milk while he chewed.

He wished his mom would hurry and call. Then he could have his snack on the run and be the first kid on the playground. Every day as he waited for her call, it seemed like he was waiting for next year.

Jerry was halfway through his sandwich and milk when the phone finally rang. He pounced on it in midring.

"Hello, Mom?"

"Yes, Jerry, it's me. Did you have a good day?"

Jerry thought his mother always sounded so businesslike when she called from the clinic. "Yeah. It was okay. About like usual." Then he remembered he had something to tell her. "I got a B+ on my spelling test."

"That's good. Did you bring the test home?"

"Um-hum." Jerry took another bite of sandwich.

"Well, you'll have to study the ones you missed. Next time, try for an A."

"Um-hum."

"Jerry, don't talk with your mouth full."

Jerry grinned. She couldn't see him but she could hear him. You couldn't fool mothers. He swallowed loudly. "Okay, Mom."

She laughed. "Well, all right, Jerry. Have fun but remember the rules."

Jerry eyed the playground rules. They were posted below the apartment rules. They were held up by four more soccer ball magnets that Jerry had given his father for his birthday in case he ever wanted to post anything on the fridge.

1- No detours. Go straight to the playground.
2- There must be at least 5 other kids on the playground.
3- Do not leave the playground until you are ready to come home.
4- You must be home 15 minutes before 5.
5- Walk home in a group.
6- No detours. Come straight home.

Underneath these rules there was a list of emergency numbers held up by four backup soccer magnets that Jerry had given his mother in case some of the others broke or got lost.

1- Mom at work - 678–9899
2- police - 222–1231
3- fire dept. - 222–7788
4- apartment super - 789–9007
5- Dr. Naggi - 678–4678
6- Grandpa and Gram - 788–5565
7- David's mom - 789–0076
8- ARO Trucking - 678–4421

There was no way he could forget all those rules and regulations, Jerry thought.

"Okay, Mom. See you tonight."

Jerry hung up the phone and finished his milk. He wiped his mouth on his sleeve, scooped up his soccer ball from the floor of the hall closet, and was turning to go when the phone rang again. Jerry turned around to answer it. His mother must have forgotten something.

CHAPTER **3**

"Hello, Mom?" Jerry said.

"Hello," said a tiny voice. It wasn't his mother.

When the voice didn't speak, Jerry said again, "Hello? Who are you calling?"

"Hello? Who is this?" said the little voice.

"Jerry." He knew he wasn't supposed to give his name over the phone. He didn't give his last name. Nobody would know who Jerry was. There could be millions of Jerrys in the city. Anyway, it was probably the little sister or brother of one of his friends.

"Hi, Jerry," the tiny voice piped with enthusiasm, as if it, whoever it was, had known Jerry forever.

"Who are you calling?" he asked.

"I'm calling you," said the little voice.

"But who are you?"

"I'm Sherita."

Jerry couldn't remember anybody named Sherita. "Are you somebody's sister?"

"No, I don't have any brothers or sisters. Do you?"

"No. Listen, if you're not somebody's sister, how'd you get this number?"

"I made it up." She giggled.

"How?" Jerry asked.

"It was easy. I just wrote down a bunch of numbers and then I dialed them."

"But why?"

"I wanted somebody to talk to."

"But you don't know me."

"Now I do."

Jerry decided not to argue with her. "Never mind," he said. "It's been nice talking to you, Sherita, but I've got to—"

"Jerry," Sherita interrupted quickly, "do you know anything about animals?"

"Well, a little. I'm in the fourth grade. And I've

13

been to the zoo. But I'm going to be la—"

"I'm in the second grade," Sherita interrupted again. "I went to the zoo once but it was a long time ago when I was little. I was scared of the bears."

"The bears can't hurt you," Jerry told her. "They are penned in. You're safe at the zoo. Now I've—"

"They might get out and follow me home," she said.

"No, they won't. The zookeepers won't let them," Jerry assured her.

"They might," she insisted.

"Not if you keep your door locked. Bears can't open locked doors."

"You don't know that."

"Yes, I do. Who ever heard of a bear opening a door? They've got better things to do. Like me. I've—"

"Like what?"

Jerry tried to think. What do bears do? "Well, they look for beehives. You don't have a beehive in your apartment, do you?"

"Noooo."

"There." Jerry was triumphant. He'd won the

14

argument. "Bears won't bother you if you don't have a beehive."

"You don't know that."

"Yes, I do."

"Uh-uh."

Jerry slumped against the wall. You couldn't win an argument with this kid even when you were right. How was he ever going to get off the phone? Jerry knew that he could just hang up and leave. But she sounded so tiny. He couldn't be mean to her. And his parents had taught him to be polite on the telephone. What could he do? He had to get off the phone or he would be late to the playground. He decided to change the subject to get her mind off bears.

"What kind of animals do you like?" he asked.

"I don't know. I haven't seen many animals."

She had just said she'd been to the zoo. What a dumb kid. But he didn't want to mention the zoo. She might start talking about bears again. "There must be some animals you like."

"Well, I like cats. Do you?"

"Sure." Jerry was glad that his ploy had worked. Now maybe he could get her to hang up. "Listen, Sherita, I've got to—"

But before he finished his sentence, she asked another question. "Do you know how many humps a camel has?"

Jerry tried to picture a camel. "Sure. A camel has two humps." He paused. "No, one. Well, some camels have one and some have two."

"That's not right. Camels have to have the same number of humps. One or two. Which is it?"

"Just what I said. Sometimes they have one hump and sometimes two."

"You don't know much," Sherita said.

"Just a minute, Sherita. I don't have time to argue about camels. I'm late for my soccer game. Anyway, this is a dumb conversation."

"It's not dumb. I have to know. It's for school. I have to answer some questions about animals. We saw a video but now I can't 'member how many humps camels have. I need help."

"Why are you bothering me about it? Ask somebody else," Jerry said. He was impatient to be off.

"I don't know anybody else," she said.

"You could ask your mother."

"I can't call her at work 'less it's a 'mergency. And she might not know."

"Don't you have a sitter?"

"No. I stay by myself."

"I'm a latchkey kid, too," Jerry said with pride.

"Do you like coming home when nobody's there?" she whispered.

"Sure," Jerry said. "It makes me feel grown up."

"Oh."

There was a long pause. Jerry was about to say good-bye when she said, "It makes me feel lonesome. That's why I call people up. I want somebody to talk to."

"That makes sense," Jerry said. That was what he would do if he were lonesome. But he had Joel and David and the rest of his gang to call.

"What about people in your class?" he suggested. "Can't you call some of them?"

"I don't know their numbers. I don't know anybody outside of school."

Jerry sighed. Surely she knew somebody in the whole world. "There must be somebody you can call, a neighbor maybe."

"No, I don't know anybody. But now I know you."

Jerry groaned. He didn't believe there was

nobody she could call. But he didn't want to risk getting into another argument with her. She had a way of winning.

Sherita asked again. "Well, do you know how many humps a camel has?"

"I'm thinking," Jerry told her. "You ask too many questions."

"But I have to ask questions if I don't know the answers. My teacher, Miss White, says we should ask questions to find out things."

Jerry brightened. He knew what to tell her now. Mrs. Brent always told his class to look things up. "You can look up *camel* in the encyclopedia. There will be a picture and you can count the humps. There might even be three humps."

"I don't have a 'cyclopedia. Do you?"

"Well, yes, but . . ."

"Look it up for me, please, Jerry," she said.

"Can't you go to the library and look it up?"

"I'm not allowed to leave the apartment," Sherita said.

"You could look it up at school tomorrow," Jerry suggested.

"I have to turn in my homework first thing in the morning."

"Hold on," Jerry said with resignation. He was

going to get this over with in a hurry.

He ran to the bookcase and got out the *C* volume of the encyclopedia. He flipped the pages as fast as he could, overshot *camel,* and had to back up. At last he found it.

"I was right," he told Sherita. "Sometimes camels have two humps, the ones that live in China or Mongolia, and if they live in Africa or western Asia they have one hump."

There was a silence. Then Sherita said, "How should I answer the question? There's only room for one answer on the line."

Jerry gritted his teeth. He was never going to get to the playground in time. "The answer doesn't have to be on the line."

"Miss White says it does. She gets onto us if we aren't neat."

"Look, Sherita, get a ruler and make a nice straight line under the line for the answer. Then write down that some camels have one hump and some have two."

"Are you sure?"

Jerry felt like pulling his hair out. "Of course, I'm sure. I'm looking at the answer right here in the encyclopedia. Don't you believe the encyclopedia?"

"The 'cyclopedia doesn't have to answer Miss White."

Jerry groaned. "Sherita, Miss White gets her questions from books like the encyclopedia."

"How do you know?"

"Because I know. I gotta go now, Sherita."

"Okay, Jerry. Can I call you up sometimes?"

"Yeah, sometimes. Now I gotta go. I'm late."

"You can call me, too. Write down my number. It's 423–2494."

Jerry wasn't going to write down her number. He couldn't think of a single reason for ever calling Sherita.

"Did you write it down?" she asked.

"Um-hum." Jerry didn't bother to hide his impatience now.

"Well, read it back to me," Sherita demanded.

"Uh . . ."

"I knew you didn't. This time, do it. It's 423–2494."

Jerry did it, just to get her out of his hair. He wrote the number on his mother's pad by the phone. Then he drew a circle around it and made x's along the circle. It looked like a tiny barbed-wire fence.

"Okay, I did it." He read the number back to

her. He knew that was the one number in the world that he would never call. "Now I gotta go. Good-bye."

Jerry hung up the phone and grabbed his soccer ball even though he knew he was too late to get to the playground first. Tank would be there for sure and that meant Jerry would have to play football instead of soccer.

"Jeeps," he said as he closed the door behind him.

CHAPTER 4

Jerry wasn't the last at the playground but he wasn't first and that was what counted. He was glad that Tank wasn't first. Tank was built like a tank and football was his game. There were always a couple of boys hanging around him. Everybody called them Tank's army.

Jerry and his friends didn't like to play football against Tank and his army. Abe didn't mind it but he preferred basketball. Scooter liked baseball. John and Ricky liked everything but football with Tank. Joel always chose soccer because he was Jerry's best friend.

The playground wasn't officially a playground. It was only a vacant lot between two tall buildings. It didn't have slides or swings or any kind of equipment, but it was better than no playground. Two poles with hoops nailed to them served as basketball nets. The poles were set at right angles to each other instead of at each end of the lot so that the rules had to be bent for a basketball game. There were no lines marking a soccer or football field, and pieces of trash marked the goals.

When Jerry arrived the game had already been decided. Abe had been the first on the playground so the game for the day was basketball.

Joel was always the referee. He was always picking up bugs and things to take home and look at under his microscope. Sometimes he even picked them up in the middle of a game. But nobody else wanted to be referee.

"Okay, sports fiends, let's play ball," Joel said.

Abe and Tank got ready to jump for the ball. They were about the same height, but Abe had longer arms. Joel blew his whistle and threw the ball up in the air. Tank and Abe jumped at the same time. Abe slapped the ball to David. The game was on.

23

David sank the first shot before Tank's army had warmed up. Tank threw the ball to one of his lieutenants who took it out and threw it right back to Tank.

Half of the army blocked Abe, while the other half blocked David as Tank dribbled toward the basket. Jerry and the other boys were free to dart around and try to steal the ball.

Tank wasn't good at basketball (or any game except football) but he still wanted to be the star. He shot an air ball. Jerry was right under the hoop waiting for it. Tank never learned.

Jerry's team passed the ball around. Ricky sent it back to Jerry on the way to the basket. David took Jerry's pass on the outside and then, before the army knew it was coming, he bounce passed it to Abe under the basket. Abe turned and made a backhanded lay-up.

Tank jerked his head and the same lieutenant took the ball out. He threw it in to Tank. The army again tried to keep Abe and David away from Tank. Jerry, with no one on him, stole the ball from Tank and passed to Abe. The army swarmed around him. Abe passed it to David in shooting range and he swished it.

Jerry knew Tank was frustrated because he had

lost the ball twice. He was careful not to get close enough for a collision. But Abe was not so lucky. Tank dribbled under his team's basket with Abe right on him. Then Tank lunged and Abe went down.

Joel's whistle shrilled. "Foul on Tank," he said.

"He ran into me," Tank argued. "I'm the one with the ball. He fouled me."

"I'm the one with the whistle, Tank. Foul on you." Joel blew his whistle again and handed the ball to Jerry.

Jerry threw it in to John. He took it down to the hoop. John passed it back to Jerry there and he buried it.

One of Tank's lieutenants finally managed to get the ball away from Tank and make a basket. Jerry was glad. He didn't like to see a team skunked, even if it was Tank's team.

"What made you so late?" Joel asked Jerry as they were walking home.

"I had a phone call," Jerry said.

"I thought maybe you weren't coming. You've been first every day this month. It was a record."

Jerry winced at that. He didn't need to be reminded that he had missed a day of soccer.

Jerry had known he was born to play soccer since he was four and his dad took him to his first soccer match. He'd loved all the action and excitement of the game just as his dad did. He'd wanted to jump right on the field and kick the ball down to the goal. It was the greatest game in the world.

They'd play soccer tomorrow, Jerry knew, if that kid didn't call him again. Sherita. It was her fault he was late. Why did she have to make up his number out of all the zillions of telephone numbers in the city?

CHAPTER **5**

"Soccer fans," the announcer shouted over the din, "you have never seen anything like what we have just witnessed today in the Arenacade. JJ has broken the all-time record of goals scored by one player in a single game! This has been an unbelievable afternoon in the annals of soccer. Fantastic! Stupendous!"

The crowd was on its feet, roaring its approval. "JJ! JJ! JJ!"

Jerry could still hear the echo of the shouts as he unlocked his apartment door after school the next day. It was his favorite sound.

He was chewing the last bite of a peanut butter and mustard sandwich when his mother called.

"Hi, Jerry."

"Everything's okay, Mom. Gotta go," he said.

"What's your hurry?"

"You know, Mom. If I get to the playground first, I get to play soccer."

"I know, Jerry. I'm only teasing."

"Awww, Mom."

"I know you're in a rush, but can you spare a second and please take the casserole for tonight out of the refrigerator for me? It's on the bottom shelf wrapped in foil. Put it in the oven and turn it on bake. The temperature is already set."

"Yeah, Mom, okay." Jerry dashed to the fridge and found the casserole.

"All done," he reported.

"Thanks, Jerry. See you tonight."

"Bye, Mom," he said into the phone. Now to get out of here before that little kid called. He was still wearing his jacket. All he had to do was grab his soccer ball and . . .

The phone rang. Jerry hesitated. He didn't want to answer it. But it might be his mom calling back. Or his dad calling from somewhere. It could be his grandmother or Aunt Ruth or . . . He picked up the phone.

"Hello?"

"Hi, Jerry. This is Sherita. What are you doing?"

Oh no! Jerry almost yelled it into the phone. But before he could answer, she was talking again so fast he had to listen carefully to understand her. "You said I could call, 'member? Do you know how to make a camel out of playclay?"

"A what? A camel? No, I—"

"I have to make an animal for my science project. Did you ever have to do that?"

"No. Sherita, I have to go to—"

Sherita interrupted. "I tried to make a camel like we talked about yesterday. One with two humps. But it looks like a dog with an elephant on its back."

Jerry had to laugh at her description. "Once I made an elephant in art class. It looked like a cat with a string hanging off its nose."

Sherita giggled. "It's hard to make things out of playclay if you're not very good at it. I'm not very good."

"Me neither. Why do you have to make a camel? That's hard."

"Everybody in the class has to make an animal. Then we have to write a report about it. I picked camels on account of you know a lot about them."

"No, I don't," Jerry protested quickly.

"But you could look it up for me."

"But I can't make it for you."

"That's true. What can I do? I'll get a bad grade if I turn in a camel that looks like a dog. And everybody will laugh at me. . . ." Her voice trailed off.

Jerry sighed. He pictured her sniffling into the phone. She was probably a skinny little kid with her top front teeth missing, big eyes, and tiny braids with bunny barrettes on the ends. She had that kind of voice. He'd better make short work of her problem so he could be on his way. This would be a snap today.

"You'll have to make an easier animal like a snake or something," he told her.

"Jimmy is doing a snake."

Jerry stood on his left foot. "How about a fish?"

"Harry is doing a fish."

"Can't you do it, too?"

"No. Miss White says everybody has to do a different one."

Seals and pandas had already been picked.

Jerry tried to think. What would be easy for a little kid to make? A lion? A giraffe? They were hard. Everything he could think of was either too hard or somebody else was doing it. He didn't want to mention bears. "What about penguins?"

"Mark is doing them."

"Did anybody choose turtles? They're pretty easy."

"Noooo, I don't think anybody did."

Jerry stood on his right foot, ready to run. "Well, then, do a turtle."

"Okay."

Jerry was relieved that he had solved her problem for today. Now he could hang up. He might still get to the playground first. "I gotta go now—" he began.

"Wait, Jerry. What color are turtles?"

"Different colors."

"What colors?" she persisted.

"Jeeps." Jerry tried to think of turtle colors. "Brown. Gray. Green. Yellow spotted. I don't know. Get a book at the library and find out. You'll have to do that anyway for your report."

There was a long pause. Jerry was about to hang up when she said, "I thought you could tell me about turtles."

31

"I don't know much about turtles, Sherita. Anyway, you're supposed to do the work. Not me."

"I'll try," Sherita said, but Jerry could hear the doubt in her voice.

"You do that. Now I gotta go. Bye."

"Bye, Jerry. Thank you."

Click. Jerry put the receiver down, picked up his soccer ball and was out the door in one continuous motion. He felt a twinge of guilt for giving Sherita the brush-off like that. He suspected he could have helped her, but he had to get to the playground.

Jerry ran as fast as he could but he was fifth. Scooter and John were first.

"We get to choose," Scooter said.

"Yeah," John echoed.

Jerry hoped they would choose soccer. "Come on, guys, let's play soccer."

"We've played soccer for a whole month," Scooter said.

"Except yesterday," Joel reminded them.

"Yeah. That was fun," said John. "Let's do it again."

"Okay with me." Abe grinned.

Tank and his army didn't look happy about the

32

choice. Jerry and Joel didn't either, but they didn't want to be classed with Tank.

"Okay," they both agreed.

Basketball was better than football with Tank. Anything was.

"You've been late twice now," Joel said to Jerry as they were walking home.

"Yeah, what's happening?" Abe asked.

"I get these calls." Jerry didn't want to explain about Sherita, not even to Joel. He didn't want anybody to know that a girl, a second-grade girl, had made him late to the playground. "How do you get rid of somebody on the phone?" he asked the group.

"Nobody ever calls me," said Scooter.

"Me neither," said John. " 'Cept my grand-mother."

"My cousin called me once," Ricky told them. "I didn't want to talk to her but my mother made me 'cause she was moving to Los Angeles. She told me she's going to be a movie star." He snorted. "She's so ugly, she'd scare Godzilla."

"I got a cousin like that," David said. "She wants to be a policeman. She'll scare the crooks to death."

"You can pretend to be the wrong number,"

Joel said, answering Jerry's question.

"Yeah!" It was brilliant. Jerry wondered why he hadn't thought of it. Next time Sherita called, he'd pretend to be a wrong number.

Jerry's mother was setting the table in the kitchen as he let himself into the apartment. He sniffed. Tuna casserole. He should have guessed. It had sour cream and mushrooms and other yucky stuff that Jerry didn't want to know about. He usually pretended it was a peanut butter and banana sandwich and swallowed it after chewing as little as possible.

Jerry leaned against the kitchen counter and took a gulp of cold milk.

"How was your day?" his mother asked.

"It was okay." As okay as a day without soccer could be. As okay as a day with a phone call from Sherita could be.

"Mom, what do you do when people call and you don't want to talk to them?"

"People you know, Jerry, or strangers?"

Jerry thought for a minute. He didn't *really know* Sherita. "Strangers, I guess."

His mother frowned. "Have you been getting crank calls?"

"No, Mom." Sherita was a phone freak but not a crank.

"Well, if you do, hang up immediately."

"Oh, I will," Jerry promised. "You can bet I will."

CHAPTER **6**

Today Jerry was sure he would be first on the playground. He had a plan. When the phone rang, he was ready.

"Hi, Jerry—" Sherita began.

Jerry took a deep breath and interrupted. "This is Geraldine, not Jerry," he said in a high voice that he hoped sounded like a girl.

"But—"

"You have the wrong number, little girl." Jerry hung up and lunged for the door, but immediately the phone rang again.

"Hi, Jerry, this is—"

"Little girl, you have the wrong number," he said in a falsetto voice.

He hung up and leaped for the door but again the phone rang. Sherita must be the world's fastest dialer, he thought. For two cents he wouldn't answer, but it might be his mother.

"Hi, Jerry—"

"Stop bothering me, you phone freak." Jerry forgot to use the high voice, but he knew he wasn't fooling Sherita.

"This is Sherita." She continued the conversation as though he hadn't spoken.

Jerry slumped by the phone. It was no use. He bet she'd keep calling him all afternoon. He might as well listen to her and get it over with.

"I made the turtle just like you told me and guess what happened?"

Jerry didn't want to know. He didn't want to talk to Sherita. He didn't want to help her with her science project.

He didn't say anything.

"Guess."

There was a long pause. Then Sherita said, "You'll never guess what happened, Jerry. One side of the turtle's shell caved in. It just fell in. Why do you suppose that happened?"

Jerry could think of several reasons. But he didn't want to get involved. Sherita was the most persistent kid he knew. It seemed that the only way to get rid of her was to change his telephone number or be rude. He knew his parents wouldn't change the number. He would have to be rude. It was the only way. He had to play soccer. He took a deep breath.

"I have to go now." He hung up without saying good-bye or even giving Sherita a chance to say good-bye. If he had, she would have kept on talking until tomorrow.

He grabbed his soccer ball and ran out of the apartment. As the door slammed he heard the phone ring again, but he was already on his way.

As he ran, Jerry felt both happy and guilty. He was happy because he hadn't been stuck on the phone a long time. Today he would be first at the playground.

Still, he felt guilty because he had hung up on Sherita. She was only a little kid. She didn't have anybody to help her with her project. But it was a choice between what she wanted and what he wanted. Jerry chose soccer.

Jerry's feet skimmed over the sidewalk as though he had grown wings where his little toes were. Soon, he forgot all about Sherita. His big toes tingled with anticipation as he thought about dribbling the soccer ball down the whole length of the playground. This was going to be his day.

Jerry turned the corner and stopped short. Tank was in the middle of the playground tossing his football high in the air and running underneath to catch it.

It wasn't possible. Jerry had run home faster than ever, cut short his conversation with Sherita, and sped to the playground. Tank couldn't move fast enough to beat him even though he lived closer than Jerry did.

"How'd you get here so fast?" he demanded.

Tank grinned. "Maybe I've been practicing my running. Football players have to run, too. It's gonna be football today."

"I can see that." Jerry threw his soccer ball down. He felt miserable and mad at the same time.

The soccer ball bounced high with the force of Jerry's throw and continued bouncing again and again. Jerry ran behind it and kicked it with fast, furious kicks all around the playground. He was out of breath when the rest of the gang arrived.

They looked at Jerry kicking the soccer ball and

at Tank throwing the football up over his head.

"Which is it?" Abe asked.

"Football," Tank gloated. His army smirked.

One reason that Jerry didn't like to play football was that he had to carry the ball a lot because he was fast. Abe had to carry it, too, because he was tall and could catch better than anybody else. It took all of the army to get Abe down, but it only took one to tackle Jerry. Everybody Tank tackled always went down. Everybody on Jerry's team tried not to get tackled by Tank.

Joel refereed, as usual. If Tank fell on him, it would kill him or break his glasses. He pulled out the whistle he wore on a string with his latchkey and blew it. "Okay, guys. Huddle."

Both teams went into a huddle even though only one was supposed to. Tank and the army won the toss so they had to huddle to decide on a play. Jerry's team had to huddle to decide what they thought Tank was going to do and what they would do about it.

"I think they'll give the ball to Tank right away," Ricky said. "They haven't played football in a long time and you know how Tank likes to hog the ball."

"All right, guys, everybody go after Tank," Abe said. "But keep your eyes on the rest of the army."

Joel blew his whistle and the two teams lined up. Tank favored an H formation he'd made up himself.

Tank carried the ball on the first play and Jerry's team piled on him, all except Abe who was covering the army.

But Tank's team made a touchdown before Jerry's team ever got the ball. Jerry tackled Tank once by himself and got dragged ten feet before John helped him.

Abe was the quarterback. After the snap, he handed off to Jerry, who almost got free. If he had, it would have been a touchdown. Ricky carried the ball on the next play and got to the end of the playground, tying the game.

Next time around, Abe again gave the ball to Jerry. Tank was waiting for him. Jerry tried to veer to the left but Tank pounced on him in a flying leap. Jerry went down with a thud on his left knee. Most of the army piled with enthusiasm on top of Tank.

Joel pulled them off, blew his whistle, and shouted, "Unnecessary roughness. Ten yard penalty."

Jerry got up stiffly. His left knee stung. He examined it. His jeans were ripped and they were new jeans. Almost new. He'd gotten them in September. His mother was going to be mad. She wouldn't buy him new ones until his next growth spurt. These would have to be patched.

Inside the hole a raw area of skin was rapidly turning bright red. When the red began to drip, Jerry decided he'd had enough football. He found his soccer ball and started home. It was against his parents' rules for him to walk home alone from the playground, but he thought this was a sort of emergency.

"Quitter!" yelled one of the army.

"Quitter!" echoed another.

Jerry glared at them. "I gotta put something on my knee. It's bleeding and I might need stitches." Soccer players had to take care of their knees. His was already throbbing and stiffening.

"Better wash it real good," Joel said. "You don't want to get blood poisoning."

Blood poisoning! Jerry thought he would faint. But as he limped home the faintness went away.

When he got home, Jerry pulled off his jeans and soaked the torn part in cold water the way he'd seen his mother do. His knee looked awful and felt worse. Remembering what Joel said, he washed the dirt and gravel off his knee. It stung, but it was nothing like the antiseptic that he dabbed on next. He knew he had to do it. If his knee got infected, his mother would never let him go back to the playground.

His knee felt like it was on fire. Jerry hopped around the bathroom in silent misery, fanning his knee to stop the burning.

Suddenly there was a loud thump right under his feet. Jerry stopped hopping. It was Mrs. Murphy, who lived in the apartment directly below. She probably thought he was playing soccer again in the apartment. Jerry had tried doing it once in rainy weather when he couldn't go outside. He had only dribbled the ball around, hardly making any noise at all. But Mrs. Murphy had complained to the super of the building. Now, whenever she thought he was doing it, she thumped on the ceiling of her apartment with her broomstick.

Jerry hoped she wouldn't tell his mother. He wasn't even dribbling this time, but he didn't want to have to explain. Then his mother would find out about his knee, and she might make him stay home from the playground.

He tiptoed over to the shower and turned it on. Maybe Mrs. Murphy would hear the running water and think he was jumping to get out of his pants to take a shower. Maybe she would think he lost his balance and fell over.

Jerry found a patch in his mother's sewing box. He hoped he had time to iron it on before she got home. He had watched her do it plenty of times.

Jerry dried the knee part of his jeans with his mother's hair dryer so the patch would stick. But the hair dryer took too long. Jerry ran the hot iron over the wet part of his jeans. Then he started on the patch.

He heard his mother's key in the front door just as he got the patch ironed on. He unplugged the iron and put it back in the pantry. She wouldn't notice it was still warm.

The door was opening. Jerry stuck the ironing board back in the closet. He grabbed his warm pants and ran to his room. Now all he had to do was find another pair to put on and he was home free.

"Jerry?" his mother called. "Are you home yet?"

Jerry hopped into his other jeans and zipped them up. "Yeah, Mom. I'm in my room."

That night Jerry had trouble falling asleep. His throbbing knee reminded him of his day. Right over his bed was his favorite soccer poster, the one of Pelé. It was the last thing he saw at night before he went to sleep and the first thing he saw when he woke up in the morning. He lay in bed staring at the soccer ball Pelé was kicking. Jerry had painted it with luminous paint so it would glow in the dark. He was never afraid with the ball up there. If he woke up in the middle of the night, he could see it shining over him like a big white moon.

Jerry thought about Sherita. She probably had a nightlight because she was afraid of bears. He shouldn't have hung up on her. Look what had happened to him since. If he hadn't hung up, maybe his knee wouldn't be keeping him awake.

It wasn't only his knee. Jerry knew that his conscience was bothering him, too. He imagined Sherita in her bed crying into her pillow, one arm around her teddy bear. No, she wouldn't have a teddy bear. She was afraid of bears, he remembered. She probably had a rabbit or a kitten, a pink one with matted fur and limp ears and a bedraggled ribbon. And one eye missing. She

45

probably called it Binky and told it all her secrets. She was probably telling it right now how that mean Jerry had hung up on her and wouldn't help her with her turtle.

The covers were heavy on Jerry's knee. He kicked off a blanket. That was better. He fell asleep and dreamed that a giant pink rabbit with soccer ball eyes was chasing him.

CHAPTER 7

"How's your knee?" Joel asked the next morning as Jerry was getting his geography book out of his desk.

"Stiff and sore. How do you know if you have blood poisoning?" Joel always knew about science things.

"You get a red line running up your leg. Do you have one?"

"I didn't this morning." Jerry thought Joel looked disappointed. "Is that all? Just a red line?"

"You'd probably have a fever, too."

47

"I guess I don't have it then," Jerry said.

"Pass your geography homework to the front," Mrs. Brent was saying.

Jerry flipped through his notebook, then his geography book. His homework wasn't there.

Mrs. Brent noticed him. "Is there a problem, Jerry?"

"I must have left it at home," he said. "It's not here."

"You don't have your homework, Jerry?"

"I did it, Mrs. Brent. Honest. I must've left it somewhere." Jerry started thinking. He had been working on the map of Africa when his mom had said it was bedtime. He'd closed the atlas and put it back in the bookcase. His homework was probably in the atlas. Jeeps!

"Very well, Jerry. But to help you remember next time, you may answer questions four, five, eight, and nine on page forty-five."

Math was next. Jerry had four problems wrong on his homework. Then Mrs. Brent gave the class a pop spelling quiz.

"This is not my day," he complained to Joel during lunch. Jerry stabbed his orange Jell-O. It quivered horribly. Jerry liked his food to lie still on his plate.

"You're probably growing," Joel told him.

"Huh? What's that have to do with anything?"

"My dad says that when things go wrong with kids, like they have accidents and forget things, they're growing. You been falling a lot lately?"

Jerry tried to remember. "I don't think so. Only yesterday."

"That doesn't count. You had Tank and the whole army on you. Even Godzilla would've fallen down."

Jerry stabbed his Jell-O again. "Yeah. I guess."

"Are you going to eat that Jell-O?"

"No. I lost my appetite. This stuff is the color of goldfish."

"People used to eat goldfish," Joel said as he scraped the Jell-O onto his plate.

"Don't tell my mother. She might want to cook some."

"Oh, they weren't cooked," Joel said.

Jerry stared at him. "You mean they ate raw goldfish?"

"Sure. It was all for fun. My granddad said back in the twenties people used to do all kinds of crazy things."

"Like what?"

"Like trying to see how many people can crowd

49

into a telephone booth," Joel said as he finished the last of the Jell-O.

"That's fun?"

"I guess you had to be there," Joel said.

"Yeah."

Jerry checked his feet in PE to see if they were growing. They looked the same size to him. His sneakers felt the same too, except maybe the left one. His left big toe seemed a lot closer to the end of his sneaker.

"Can one toe grow but not the rest of your foot?" he asked Joel on the way back to their classroom.

"I don't think so," Joel said. "I think your whole foot has to grow at the same time."

Jerry didn't fall down as he ran home, not even with his knee stiff and sore. But suddenly, a car came out of nowhere and crushed the can he was kicking. Jerry stood on the curb and watched. The car sped away, leaving the flattened can lying in the street. Jerry felt as though that can had been his pet and he wanted to take it home and bury it in his backyard. Except he didn't have one.

Jerry didn't bother to look for another can. With his luck it would get mashed by a Mack truck. Anyway, today he wanted to concentrate on getting right to the playground.

But his bad luck held. First, there weren't any bananas. Then, before he was halfway through his peanut butter and applesauce sandwich, the telephone rang for the second time. His mother had already called. He knew she wasn't calling back. But she might be. He had to answer it. The peanut butter made a huge unswallowable lump in his mouth. Jerry let the phone ring again as he rolled the lump around in his mouth. With a mighty gulp, he forced it down and answered the phone.

"Hi, Jerry, this is Sherita. We got cut off yesterday. I tried to call you back but nobody was there. Do you 'member what happened to my turtle?" Without waiting for his reply, she went on, "It went flat. It looks like somebody sat on it and the tail fell off. What can I do to fix it? I have to take it to school on Monday."

Sherita didn't seem to realize that Jerry had hung up on her the day before. It made him feel like the meanest kid in the world.

"That's no problem, Sherita. You can glue the tail back on. And this can be a flat turtle."

"Are there flat turtles, Jerry?" There was doubt

51

in her voice. "I never saw any pictures of flat turtles."

"Yours can be flat," Jerry said.

"But if real turtles aren't flat, I don't want my turtle to be flat."

"It's okay to make a flat turtle," Jerry insisted. He chewed his peanut butter. It felt like a lump of guilt going down his gullet. He figured it was about halfway to his stomach now. It wouldn't seem to go any further. Maybe it was stuck.

"How can I fix my turtle, Jerry?"

Maybe if he jumped up and down the lump would go down.

"Are you there, Jerry?"

"Yeah, I'm still here." Jerry jumped. Nothing happened.

"You sound funny, Jerry."

Jerry jumped up and down as he talked. "I'm okay. Listen, Sherita, I'm sorry about yesterday."

"But what about my turtle?"

"Let me think."

Jerry bounced as he thought. But all he could think about was the lump somewhere below his chest. He couldn't worry about a collapsed turtle.

"Are you still thinking, Jerry?"

"Yeah." What would happen to him if the lump

52

didn't ever go down? Would it stay soft? Would other food stick to it until it filled up his insides? Would it turn to stone? It felt like a rock.

"Have you thought of anything yet, Jerry?"

Jerry had thought of something. "Sherita, do you have any rocks?"

"No, do you?"

"Sure. That's what you can use to fix your turtle."

"Rocks?" Sherita sounded doubtful.

"No, one rock. A round one. You can put your playclay over it and it won't sag or collapse." Jerry knew he had solved Sherita's problem. Now he could go to the playground. He hadn't lost much time yet.

"But I don't have a rock."

"Do you live near a park or a playground?"

"No, not very near."

"Tomorrow's Saturday. Couldn't your mother take you to a park so you can find a rock for your science project?" Jerry asked with desperation. How was he going to get off the phone? After yesterday, he could never hang up on her again.

"Well, I guess so. I can ask her."

"That's great. You can make a great turtle. I gotta go play soccer now."

"Are you on a soccer team?"

"No, but I'm planning to be in the spring. That's why I have to practice. Your problem is taken care of now and I gotta go play soccer."

"Where do you practice?"

"At the playground."

"Which playground?"

"It's not really a playground, just an empty lot. Now I've—"

"What empty lot?" Sherita demanded.

Jerry had never known anybody who asked so many questions. If trees could talk, Sherita would probably ask them where their roots go. Why did she want to know where his playground was? But he knew better than to answer her question with a question. "It's on Vine Street."

"Where on Vine Street?"

"Between Post and General MacArthur Boulevard. Now I've got to go. The guys will all—"

"Okay, Jerry," she interrupted him. "Bye."

To his amazement, she hung up. Jerry didn't believe in questioning his good luck. He hung up, too, and rushed out of the apartment. As he ran, the peanut butter lump dropped. Then it disappeared, and Jerry felt great.

CHAPTER

Jerry figured he must have broken some records to get to the playground first, even after talking to Sherita.

"It's gonna be soccer today, sports fans," he yelled happily as the first of Tank's army arrived.

Jerry's team won the toss. Ricky took the ball out and kicked it straight to Jerry. The army was all around him, yelping like a pack of hounds as Jerry worked his way down the field, guarding the ball from their darting feet. All he needed was one clear kick. Their goalie was slow.

Jerry watched for an opening. He took deep

gulps of air. He felt alive all over. Even his hair felt alive. This was what he was born for . . . guarding, running, planning, being on his own with the ball, Jerry couldn't imagine anything more fun. It was the greatest feeling in the world.

Jerry lofted the ball over two fallen army players before they could scramble to their feet. Ricky picked it up and passed it to John, who passed it back to Jerry before Tank and his team could decide who had the ball. Now Jerry had his opening. He let fly with a tremendous kick.

Their goalie had planted his feet in the middle of the cage. Jerry kicked the ball to the far right. The goalie lunged, but not far or fast enough, and the ball hit the side of the building behind him with a satisfying smack that sounded better than music to Jerry's ears.

Tank's lieutenant took the ball out. He aimed it straight at Tank, but Jerry was waiting for it. He snagged the ball, dribbled it downfield, and made another goal before the army knew they'd lost the ball. The goalie lunged for it, but tripped over his shoelace. "No fair," he said.

"It is fair," Joel said as he blew his whistle. "Players are responsible for their equipment. That means shoelaces. Hurry up and get it tied."

The goalie made a big show of tying a double knot. Then he tied the other one the same way. Just as he jerked it tight, Jerry saw something out of the corner of his eye, something small with pigtails.

He turned and saw a little girl standing on the sidewalk.

This time Tank took the ball out. He passed it to his lieutenant, but Jerry darted by and snagged it again. As he dribbled downfield in a zigzag pattern, he came closer to the little girl. He thought she was about the size of a second grader. She was watching the game.

Someone zipped the ball away from Jerry. Jerry's attention snapped back to the game. He tore out in pursuit, caught up, and kicked out before the other player could defend the ball. Ricky was there to pick it up and take it to the goal.

Jerry looked back at the kid. It couldn't be, he thought. It had to be a coincidence. Sherita wouldn't have come to his playground.

"Time out," he called, and ran over to check.

"Are you Jerry?" she asked.

"Sherita?" She was wearing a red sweatshirt with a kitten on the front and green corduroys with a ladybug on one knee. Her black hair was in braids that ended in plastic kitten barrettes. She had light brown skin and lively brown eyes. She grinned at him, and he saw the hole where her front teeth were missing. "Oh, no, Sherita," he groaned. "What are you doing here?"

"I wanted to see you, Jerry."

"But how did you get here?"

"I came on the bus. It comes right down General MacArthur Boulevard. I ride it with my mother when we go to the library on Saturdays."

"Sherita, aren't you supposed to stay in your apartment after school?" Jerry asked. He knew that was her mother's rule.

"Yes." She looked down at her feet. She wore red sneakers. There was a tiny hole in the toe of the left one.

What was he going to do with her? She was too little to be running around loose in the city. "You can't stay here, Sherita. It's getting late. You'll have to go back home."

"But I just got here, Jerry. Can't I stay with you?" She looked up at him.

Jerry groaned. Why did she have to have such big brown eyes and be so little? He glanced around. It was getting late. There was no bus that went straight back up MacArthur. She would have to change at least once on the return trip. Jerry looked back at Sherita. She was still watching him, waiting for him to tell her what to do.

She was so trusting. Jerry knew what he had to do. He didn't want to but he had to. He couldn't send Sherita off on a bunch of buses by herself. She might get lost or kidnapped. She might ride the wrong bus and be halfway to Canada before she even knew it.

Why me? he thought. Why did she have to pick me? And why today? Today when he was at last playing soccer again? Jerry stood for a minute, putting off the decision to end his soccer game. "Wait here," he told her. Then he walked back to the two teams, who were watching him.

"I've got to go," he said. The words felt like rocks pelting him. "I can't finish the game. You can play basketball if you want to change games."

"Why?" asked Joel.

"I've gotta take her home," Jerry said without enthusiasm.

Tank's friends erupted with yells and whistles. "Jerry's got a girlfriend!" Tank said, snickering.

"Don't be dumb," Jerry said. He picked up his soccer ball and walked back to Sherita as the guys chanted, "Jerry's got a girlfriend."

Jerry looked at Joel and shrugged. Joel and Jerry's other friends stared. He knew they didn't know what to think. They knew he would never leave a soccer game unless both of his legs were broken or something else was really wrong.

"Come on," he said to Sherita. "I'll take you home."

At first Jerry planned to take Sherita only as far as her second bus stop. But as they walked to the first one, she slipped her hand into his. She seemed so sure that he would take care of her. It gave him a funny feeling. He knew he would have to take her all the way to her building.

He dug into his pocket as they waited at the bus stop. It was lucky he had some change, he thought. He had enough for their fares and his coming back.

"You shouldn't have come here, Sherita," Jerry said when they were on the bus.

"I wanted to see what you look like." She grinned and showed the gap where her front teeth were missing.

"I know your mother wouldn't like it."

"I won't tell her."

"What if she calls up and you aren't there?

She might call the police," Jerry said.

"I never thought about that. But she only calls once."

"She might call again."

"Aren't you glad to see me a little?"

"That has nothing to do with it," Jerry said. He was irritated that she just did what she wanted to do without thinking about what might happen. "We could both get into a lot of trouble. And you kept me from doing what I like to do more than anything in the world."

"What's that?"

"Play soccer."

"I'm sorry, Jerry."

Her eyes seemed to grow bigger. A fat tear overflowed from the corner of one. She sniffed.

Oh no, Jerry thought. Not that. "It's all right, Sherita. Don't cry. I'm glad uh . . ." he stopped. He couldn't say he was glad she came and interrupted his soccer game and made him feel responsible for her so he had to give up his game and take her home. He couldn't say he was glad that he might be late getting home, and his mother would find out that he had left the playground and gone across the city on buses, which was against all the rules on the refrigerator. But he knew he had to say something to comfort Sherita and stop her from crying.

"Um, I'm glad that we finally got to meet," he said.

"Are you really, Jerry?"

"Yes, I am," he said as she looked up at him with shining eyes. It wasn't totally untrue. He had wondered what she looked like, too, and now he knew. She looked exactly as he had thought she would. Only she was smaller and not as bossy.

Jerry wished the bus would hurry. Rush hour was starting now and traffic would be slower going home. But at last they reached her apartment building. "Go straight up to your apartment now," he told her as he turned to go back to the bus stop.

"Can I still call you up, Jerry?" she called after him.

Jerry froze. How could he say no?

"Okay, sure, Sherita. You can still call me up sometimes."

"Bye, Jerry."

"Bye." Jerry headed back down the street toward the bus stop. He didn't have to turn his head to see her. A picture of her was glued behind his eyelids. He had been face-to-face with her and hadn't told her not to call him up. In fact, he had told her to call him sometime. Plus he could be in big trouble if his mother found out he had left the playground. So why did he feel so good?

CHAPTER 9

The streets were crowded with rush hour traffic by the time Jerry got back on the bus. The sky had that murky purple look it got just before dusk, and there were deep shadows between the buildings. It would be dark before he got home.

Jerry was worried. He knew he was going to be late. If his mom got home before he did, she might think something had happened to him. She might even call the police.

The bus crept down General MacArthur Boulevard, stopping at each corner to let a few people off and more passengers on. There were people standing in the aisles holding onto straps, the backs of seats, each other; people going home from work, just like his mom. Maybe she was caught in a traffic jam, too, he thought, hoping it was so.

The bus lurched forward a few feet, then came to another standstill. Horns blared but traffic didn't move. Minutes passed as Jerry watched the daylight disappearing. He couldn't sit on this bus all night. He had to do something.

Jerry jumped up and pulled the cord to be let off. He squeezed through the passengers to the back door but the door was closed. The bus driver wouldn't open it until the next stop. It was so close. Jerry could see the red sign with the white letters spelling BUS STOP just ahead.

The bus moved an inch. Jerry let out a sigh of relief. Then the bus stopped again. It moved another inch. Then it stopped. Jerry thought if he ever got off this bus, he would never stop running.

The bus finally rolled to the stop. The door opened. Jerry burst out and hit the ground at a run. He sprinted until he reached his building. He sped up the stairs and down the hall. He slowed down as he approached his door. He put his key in the lock and turned it gently. He opened the door.

The light was on in the kitchen. He hadn't left it on. That meant his mother was home.

"Jerry, where have you been?"

She didn't sound upset, Jerry thought.

Then she came out of the kitchen. She had the telephone receiver in her hand.

That was a bad sign. "I've been to the playground," Jerry said.

His mother gave him the look that meant she knew he wasn't telling all of the truth. She hung the receiver up. "Your friends have been home from the playground for over an hour. You have some explaining to do. Where have you been?"

Jerry began to tell her about Sherita. "There's this little girl. She followed me to the playground. She's only seven, real little. You wouldn't believe how little she is. She could probably pass for four. I had to take her home. The bus got stuck in traffic. That's why I'm late."

"I see." Jerry was glad that his mother didn't look angry. She picked up the pot holder shaped like a soccer ball he'd given her for Mother's Day. She opened the oven door and looked in. Then she turned back to Jerry.

He waited, afraid of what was coming.

"You felt responsible for this little girl. I'm glad that you were, Jerry. But you should have brought her home with you. We could have called her parents and made arrangements to take her home."

"I think she only has a mother."

"We could have called her mother."

"I didn't think about that," Jerry said.

"That's the problem, Jerry. You didn't think. That's why your dad and I made these rules. You have to follow them. When you are older, you can make your own rules. By then, maybe you will have learned to think things out."

Jerry listened to his mother with a sinking heart. He knew he was going to be punished. But how?

"Until then," his mother went on, "you will have to abide by our rules. I'll discuss the details with your dad when he calls. Now give me your door key."

Jerry froze. Not his latchkey. Surely she wouldn't take away his latchkey.

His mother held out her hand. "Come on, Jerry. We told you what would happen if you disobeyed the rules."

Slowly Jerry slipped the chain over his head. He felt as though he were underwater looking up at the world. The key banged against his nose the way it always did when he took it off. He held it out to his mother.

"Is it forever?" he asked, almost choking on the words.

"I'll discuss it with your father. Go and wash up now for supper."

Jerry wasn't hungry. He didn't think he would ever be hungry again. And if he had been hungry, he wouldn't have wanted tuna loaf with broccoli in it. Yucko. He pushed the green mess around on his plate. Why were so many bad things green? Jerry had nothing against the color. It was nice for grass and leaves and leprechauns. But not for food. Except for gumdrops and lollipops and M & M's.

In the middle of supper the phone rang. Jerry jumped, but it was somebody from his mother's office inviting her to a bridal shower. They talked for so long that Jerry was able to scrape and rinse his plate without his mother noticing that he had eaten less than three bites.

He mumbled something about studying and went to his room. He closed the door behind him.

He wanted to get away from the smell of the tuna loaf, he told himself. But he also wanted to hide from the world.

Jerry sat on the edge of his bed. His arms hung down, dangling between his knees. He stared at his wall of posters and clippings, a jumble of colors and newsprint. What was he going to do now?

He had tried to do the right thing about Sherita. It had seemed right at the time. If only the buses hadn't been so slow.

If only Sherita had dialed one different digit, she would have gotten somebody else on the phone.

If only he had hung up on her the first time she called.

If only . . .

But Jerry knew there was nothing to be gained by if onlys. He had taken Sherita home, but in doing it he had gotten himself in the worst trouble he'd ever been in. Now all he could do was wait for his dad to call.

It seemed to Jerry that the phone had never rung so much. It rang more that night than it usually did in a week.

The first call after supper was Joel.

"What happened, Jerry? Who was that little girl?"

Jerry explained. "She's just a kid I know, the one who has been calling me. I had to take her home and then the bus was late. I'm in big trouble."

"Yeah, I know. Your mom called my mom looking for you. What are they going to do to you?"

"She took my latchkey," Jerry whispered the words. He couldn't say them out loud.

"For how long?"

"I don't know yet. She's got to talk to Dad. He's supposed to call tonight. I better get off the phone."

"Okay."

When the phone rang again, Jerry thought it might be one of his gang. But it was one of Tank's lieutenants. He sniggered, "Jerry's got a girlfriend," then hung up before Jerry could tell which one it was. Jerry felt like bashing the telephone into every one of those guys.

The next call was the one he'd been dreading, his father calling from Omaha. Jerry waited in the living room. His mother had taken his latchkey away, maybe forever. He waited to hear what else his parents would do to him.

After what seemed like three years, his mother came in and sat down. "That was Dad. He was in a rush and only had a few minutes to talk. He agrees with me that you used poor judgment. You have to understand that the rules are not to be broken."

"I didn't mean to break the rules," Jerry protested. "I just didn't know what else to do."

"We know that, Jerry. But you did break them. So we have decided that for one week you will go to a sitter."

It was worse than Jerry had thought. "Who?"

"Mr. Burt Feeney."

"Who is he?"

"You've met him. He used to work at Dad's company."

"I don't remember him. Was he a driver?"

"No, he was a checker. He's retired now. Dad has given him rides to his daughter's house for visits from time to time. He says he will be glad for your company this week. Actually, it is working out quite well. He only lives three blocks from here, closer to the school than we do."

It wasn't working out well for Jerry. He hardly dared to ask. "Can I still go to the playground then?"

"No, Jerry. You must go straight to Mr. Feeney's house and stay there. After a week of punishment, maybe you will remember that the rules are to be obeyed. This is really important, Jerry. Do you understand?"

Jerry nodded. He understood. He had no hope now. He had been sentenced to a week without soccer. A whole week. Maybe the last week before winter. Now he would never be a soccer star.

CHAPTER 10

Monday morning was a clear, crisply cold day, a perfect day for soccer. Jerry felt only half dressed without his latchkey under his shirt. He couldn't let anybody know he wasn't a latchkey kid anymore. It was too humiliating. He imagined the army's jeers as he tied his sneakers. "Mama's baby" was probably the nicest of them.

They wouldn't find out. Not if he could help it. Jerry rummaged in his top drawer until he found an old key. He slipped it onto a shoelace, knotted the ends around his neck, and dropped the key under his shirt. He looked in the mirror. It was smaller than his real latchkey, but hopefully no-body would notice the difference. If anybody did, Jerry planned to say that his lock had been changed.

But he, Jerry, would know. The old key didn't feel like his latchkey. It felt like a stone hung around his neck.

Then there was the problem of the playground. How was he going to explain his absence to the army?

"Tell them I've gone to the dentist," Jerry told Joel at school.

"All week?"

"I guess so."

"But nobody goes every day for a week," Joel objected.

"Well, make up something. Tell them my grandmother is here or something."

Joel looked doubtful. "I'll try."

After school Jerry went to the address his mother had given him. He walked slowly along the sidewalk. He was in no hurry to get there. His mother had said he had met Mr. Feeney, but Jerry didn't remember him. It must have been while he was still a baby.

Jerry kicked a Coke can for a while. But it was

no fun unless he could run and lift the can and race with it as it spun high overhead. What was the use of doing that if his soccer career was already over? When the can rolled into the gutter, Jerry left it there.

The apartment building looked a lot like Jerry's. Mr. Feeney lived on the third floor. Jerry climbed the stairs and went down a dark hall until he found number six. There was a brass card holder on the door. A card in it said B. F. FEENEY. Jerry knocked.

"No need to bang. I can still hear as well as you can," said the man who opened the door on Jerry's third knock.

He was a thin old man with sparse gray hair. He wore gray wool pants and a gray cardigan sweater over a gray and blue plaid shirt. On his nose were thick-lensed glasses with black rims. "Come in, boy. Don't let the heat out."

Jerry went in. The apartment smelled like medicine. It was dark. All the blinds on the windows were closed. Jerry tripped over something that felt like a footstool, but it could have been a giant mushroom.

"Watch where you're going, boy," Mr. Feeney said.

The living room was lit by a large TV screen. "Marsha, you must listen to me," an actor was saying. "Phillip, darling, it's for the best," an actress replied.

Mr. Feeney went back to his chair, an overstuffed armchair with a fat ottoman in front of it for his feet.

"Mr. Feeney," Jerry began.

"Ssshhh, I want to hear this," Mr. Feeney interrupted.

Jerry had meant to ask him where he should do his homework. As his eyes adjusted to the dark, he saw that this was a one-room apartment, a studio apartment. There was nowhere else to go but the bathroom. Jerry sat down on the edge of a hard sofa. What was he supposed to do now?"

When the commercial came on, Mr. Feeney turned to Jerry. "Now then, I suppose you'd like a snack?"

This was better. "Yes sir, I would."

"Good." Mr. Feeney went to the kitchen alcove. Jerry noticed that his feet were in bedroom boots, the kind that are lined with fake furry stuff.

Mr. Feeney made noises in the kitchen. He came back in a few seconds with a saucer. On it were two halves of an apple. He took one and offered the other to Jerry. "Boy needs a snack after school," he said almost to himself. "I know I always did."

Jerry ate his apple half right away. He was always hungry after school. Mr. Feeney nibbled his half for the rest of the afternoon, in between doses of cough syrup, lozenges, and nasal spray. His medicines were crowded on a small table at his elbow. Jerry thought he must have half a drugstore there.

The telephone was on the table, too. When it rang, Mr. Feeney answered with a loud, "Hello? Who? Yes, he's here. You want to speak to him?"

He handed the receiver to Jerry. "It's your mother."

"Hi, Mom," Jerry said without enthusiasm.

"Hello, Jerry. I'm just checking to see that you got there safely. Everything all right?"

"Sure, Mom. Just great."

"It's not forever, Jerry."

"I know." Jerry said good-bye and hung up. It was forever to him.

The TV program came to an end. Jerry hoped something good would come on now. Maybe a sports program.

After a string of commercials, organ music

oozed from the TV. An announcer said, "Hospital Hearts," as the screen showed a hand putting a stethoscope on lacy valentine hearts. Jerry couldn't believe anybody would watch this.

He wished he could talk to somebody, anybody. He even wished he could talk to Sherita. Maybe he could call her. He could tell her how she'd got him into trouble.

"May I use your telephone, Mr. Feeney?" he asked during a commercial.

"Is it an emergency?"

"No, I guess not."

"Then the answer is no. I have basic budget service and pay for every call."

Jerry sank back on the sofa. He would have to wait it out. His friends were all out on the playground. He was stuck here in soap opera land with the stingiest man in the world. Jerry had never heard of giving somebody half of an apple. He could see a banana sticking up in a fruit bowl on the counter in the kitchen. Jerry's mouth watered for that banana.

There was nothing to do but watch TV. Jerry's attention was drawn into "Hospital Hearts" against his will. He found himself watching Dr. Valentine Monroe, who was being sued for malpractice by Arlene Alewine because she had a tiny scar on her throat after nearly choking on a canapé of caviar. Jerry didn't know what a canapé of caviar was but he planned never to eat one. Dr. Monroe saved Arlene but Arlene was suing anyway because her lawyer Michael was in love with Dr. Monroe. Arlene wanted him to be in love with her. Michael's ex-wife Carlotta was in love with Dr. Joel Mansfield who wanted to marry Dr. Monroe. Dr. Mansfield used to be married to Arlene, too. Later he was married to Melissa Talbot, a therapist, but now she was married to Dr. James Turner. There was something mysterious about Dr. Turner but nobody knew what it was except that it had happened in medical school.

Jerry figured it out. Dr. Turner had probably secretly been married to Dr. Monroe and had never gotten divorced. That's why he acted so strangely.

"Hospital Hearts" ended with Dr. Turner hiding in a closet while Dr. Monroe walked by with Michael.

Next came "The Sands of Time." It opened with a sand dune blowing around in the wind while waves lashed it furiously. Dorothea was in love with Archer Breckinridge, whose ex-wife

Avis vowed she was going to get him back or else. Archer's secretary Iris was spying on him for Avis because she was in love with Avis's brother Tony who was blackmailing his sister because she once did something terrible.

Jerry thought the terrible thing she did was wear two-foot-long fake eyelashes and blink them all the time. She was driving him crazy with her whiny voice and batting eyelashes.

Jerry was glassy eyed when his mother called for him to come home. How was he going to stand a week of this?

The next day Jerry packed a survival kit. He put in a snack, which he ate on the way to Mr. Feeney's. He also put in a flashlight to do his homework by, but Mr. Feeney said it bothered his eyes. So every day Jerry had to listen to the problems of the soap opera people.

Mr. Feeney had told Jerry's mother that he would be glad of Jerry's company. But Jerry thought the soap opera people were all the company Mr. Feeney needed. He didn't talk to Jerry. He talked to the soap opera people. He would nod when one of them said something he agreed with or he would say things like, "That's telling her," or "Don't go in there," or "Don't listen to him, Dr. Monroe," or "Watch out for Archer."

Mr. Feeney had a subscription to a magazine called *TV Chronicles*. It told all about the actors playing the parts and summarized all the episodes in case you had to go to the dentist and missed an episode.

"You wouldn't believe this guy," Jerry exploded to Joel on the phone that night. "All he ever does besides watch these shows on TV is suck on cough drops. Today he told me he was seriously getting a sore throat. He wore two mufflers around his neck. He looked like a skinny turtle!"

"My grandmother is like that. She wears a muffler around her nose sometimes. She watches the soap operas, too. Once my uncle was sick while he was staying with her. He got hooked and when he went home, he started taping them on his VCR while he was at work so he could watch them when he got home."

"Yuck. Grown-ups are weird. I don't know why they don't like cartoons."

"Yeah," Joel agreed.

"How am I going to get through a whole week?" Jerry moaned.

It was the longest week of Jerry's life. And when it ended, Dr. Monroe was locked in the X-ray room, Iris was locked in a closet in Archer's hunting lodge, Dorothea was locked in a tiger cage with the tiger in it, and Dr. Turner had fallen over a waterfall.

As Jerry was putting on his jacket Mr. Feeney said, "To celebrate the end of your week with me, I bought a special treat for you." He held out a small white paper bag to Jerry.

"Thanks, Mr. Feeney." Jerry looked inside. At first he thought Mr. Feeney had given him a bag of goldfish. Then he saw that the goldfish were four pieces of that awful orange slice candy, the kind that is sugary on the outside and horribly slimy on the inside.

Mr. Feeney watched with an expectant look. Jerry took out a slice of the candy. He bit through the gritty sweet coating, then swallowed the bite whole without chewing.

"Have one, Mr. Feeney." He offered the bag.

"No, boy. These are all for you," Mr. Feeney said. He was smiling. Jerry had never seen him smile before.

"They're awfully good," Jerry said. He took another bite.

"That was my favorite candy when I was a boy," Mr. Feeney said. "We used to ride into town every Saturday in the wagon behind our old mule, Red. Momma would give us a nickel for candy for all of us. These orange slices were the most you could get for a nickel. We each got half a slice."

The orange bite stuck in Jerry's throat. He didn't know what to say. He couldn't imagine Mr. Feeney as a little boy riding all the way to town and only getting half of an orange slice.

He swallowed hard. "Well, thanks again, Mr. Feeney. This is real good candy. I'll just save the rest for after supper. Mom doesn't like for me to eat this close to supper."

"Quite right. I don't know what I was thinking of." Mr. Feeney smiled at Jerry. The wrinkles on his cheeks rode up to his eyes and made him look even more like a turtle. "I enjoyed your company this week, Jerry." But as Jerry was going out the door Mr. Feeney said, "I can't wait until next week to find out what happened to all my friends. If you want to know, you can give a call."

Jerry said good-bye. He didn't tell Mr. Feeney that he hoped he, Jerry, never found out what happened.

CHAPTER **11**

Jerry ran on air all the way home from Mr. Feeney's.

"Faster than the speed of light, sports fans!" gasped the announcer.

Jerry raced up the stairs to his floor. The wonderful smell of hamburgers reached him as soon as he stepped into the hall. He followed the trail of hamburger smell all the way to his door. His mother never cooked hamburgers. It meant his dad was home.

The door wasn't locked. Jerry flung it open. "Dad!" he yelled happily.

His father was in the kitchen. He was a tall man with dark hair and brown eyes like Jerry's. He wore a blue denim apron over his jeans and plaid shirt, the sleeves rolled to the elbows. On the apron in big red letters it said: MAN IN THE KITCHEN. Jerry grabbed him around the waist in a bear hug.

"Hold on there, sport," his father said, laughing. "Let me flip this burger."

He turned the burger over with an oversized spatula and then grabbed Jerry and hugged him back.

"Jeeps, Dad, this has been an awful week." Jerry told him about Mr. Feeney, but his dad didn't seem to think it was so awful. He laughed.

"What an experience, Jerry. Bert was always worried about his health. I remember him sucking those awful-smelling cough drops when he went with me on cross-country hauls. It was like having a hospital in the cab with me."

"He has a whole drugstore on the table by his chair," Jerry said. "All week he only gave me half of an apple for a snack. Then when I was leaving today he gave me this bag of orange candy. Next to licorice, it's the worst candy in the world. He says it's his favorite."

Jerry's dad laughed. "I should go to see Bert. He and Dotty fed me a lot of meals before I married your mother. Trouble is, I'm home so little that I like to spend my time with my family. Maybe you and I can go to see him one day, Jerry."

Jerry hoped it wouldn't be too soon. Mr. Feeney would probably want to catch him up on everything that had happened on the soap operas. "Not this weekend. I need to play soccer. I didn't get to play all week. My muscles are all soft from sitting on Mr. Feeney's sofa. I need a workout."

"I guess you do. That reminds me, I have something that belongs to you."

His father opened a drawer in the kitchen and took out a key, Jerry's key. "You'll be needing this."

Jerry took the key but he didn't put it on. He didn't want his father to see the other key around his neck. He put the latchkey in his pocket and kept his hand on it for a long time, curling his fingers around the key, feeling its shape pressed against his palm. He never wanted to lose his latchkey again.

"Next time," his father said, "think before you break the rules. Now how about some supper?"

Jerry gave him another hug. He was glad his dad wasn't going to give him a lecture. "Jeeps, I'm glad you're home, Dad. Mom has been feeding me tuna fish every night almost."

His dad ruffled Jerry's hair. "Nothing wrong with tuna. It's good for the brain. It should improve your schoolwork a lot."

"Yeah, Dad," Jerry said. "But not my taste buds. I've been hungry for a hamburger."

"Soccer players need red meat, huh?"

"They sure do. I wish you'd tell that to Mom."

"She thinks fish is just as good for you," his dad said as he turned the burgers again.

"She'll be sorry when I start growing fins," Jerry said. "When can we eat?"

"Soon as your mother gets home." His father checked his watch. "Which should be any minute now. How about setting the table?"

"Okay." Jerry went to wash his hands. His heart felt as light as his feet. It was going to be a great weekend.

On Saturday, Jerry and his dad kicked the ball around the playground. And on Sunday, they went to a soccer game at City College. Jerry jumped as he watched the players. His knees twitched and his toes itched to be out there running and kicking the ball, too. There was nothing in the world as great as playing soccer. Except being with his dad at a soccer game.

Jerry's latchkey bumped agreeably beneath his shirt as he ran to school on Monday. It felt much better than the substitute key. He pulled his key out before class started and checked the clasp on the chain. He knew the clasp was okay but he wanted people to see his key. Joel gave him a thumbs-up sign from across the room.

Jerry hadn't talked to Sherita since the day he had taken her home. He had almost forgotten about her during his week with Mr. Feeney. His problems had taken all his attention. He was surprised when she called after school. Surely she would have given up after a week with nobody answering the phone at his house. Anybody else would. But not Sherita. She never gave up. Jerry knew he should have called her and told her what had happened and why he hadn't been home. But he had been so miserable.

"Hi, Jerry. This is Sherita. Where have you been?"

"I had to go to a sitter all last week. I was being punished for taking you home. I didn't get to play soccer all week." And it was all your fault, his tone implied.

"I'm sorry, Jerry. Honest."

"Why'd you do it?"

"I just wanted to meet you. I didn't mean to get you in trouble." She sounded like she was going to cry.

"That's okay, Sherita. Just don't do it again."

"I won't," she sniffled. "Thank you for taking me home."

"I said it's okay, Sherita. Uh, how's your turtle project?"

"That's why I called. I need to know some things about turtles. Where do they sleep?"

Didn't she know anything? "In their shells," Jerry replied, biting off the "stupid" he wanted to add.

"But where are their shells when they are sleeping? In the water? Or do they burrow in mud? Or what?"

"Jeeps, I don't know. Get a book and find out." Sherita asked more questions than anybody he'd ever met. He bet she stayed awake all night thinking them up. But he had to admit she never gave up. And he never knew what she was going to ask him next.

"Can't you look in your 'cyclopedia for me?"

"No, I can't," Jerry told her. "I need to play soccer. I didn't get to play all last week. I have to go now."

But not before he checked the encyclopedia for the sleeping habits of turtles.

It seemed that nothing had changed with Sherita. She was as determined as ever to keep Jerry on the phone and make him miss soccer. She seemed to think he knew the answers to everything and if he didn't, he would find out for her. She depended on him to help her. Jerry had to help her. He couldn't let her down.

Jerry didn't have a brother or sister, but now he thought he knew what it was like to be a big brother. Sherita had sort of adopted him to be hers.

He decided to ask her a question. "Sherita, why do you call me up every day and ask me all these questions?"

" 'Cause I need help on my project."

Jerry had a feeling that there was something more behind it. "You can ask the school librarian to help you," he said.

Sherita didn't say anything.

"I mean, maybe the librarian couldn't tell you

how to make a playclay turtle, but she could help you find a book about turtles that would have all the answers in it."

Still Sherita didn't reply.

"You're not being fair, Sherita. I've answered your questions. Now you have to answer mine. Why do you call me up every day at the same time?"

" 'Cause I'm scared."

Scared? What could she be scared of? "You weren't scared to take the bus all by yourself to the playground."

"That's different. There were people around. Aren't you scared?"

"No. Why should I be?"

"Is anybody home when you get there?"

"No. Nobody's here."

"Nobody's here when I come home and it's scary," she whispered.

"Why is it scary?" Jerry asked. "Why are you whispering?"

"It's so quiet. And empty. And something might be there," she finished in a rush.

"What do you mean, something might be there?" Jerry was puzzled. What was the matter with Sherita?

"You know, bears or burglars or something."

So that was it. "Aw, Sherita, you're imagining things. There's nothing to be afraid of. If your apartment is empty, that means nobody is there and you're safe," Jerry told her with what he thought was perfect logic.

"I didn't say somebody might be there. I said some*thing,*" Sherita corrected him, "or bears or burglars. That's not somebody."

"Same thing," Jerry said. "It's all your imagination. Why don't you turn on the TV? Then there will be voices and you won't feel alone." He thought of Mr. Feeney.

"Our TV's broke. It's at the shop getting fixed but it's taking a long time."

"How about a radio then?" he suggested.

"I don't have one."

She didn't have a tape player either. She didn't even have a wind-up musical toy. Jerry ran out of suggestions. He was also running out of time, he thought, as he noticed the kitchen clock. Jerry didn't quite know why but he felt that it was his responsibility to solve Sherita's problem about being scared. Of all the telephone numbers in the city, she had picked his. It was almost as though she had especially chosen him to protect her from the monsters of her imagination. But he didn't know how. Just talking on the phone every day wasn't really the answer. He couldn't talk to her every day until her mother came home. That wasn't it. And besides, he had his own things to do.

"I guess I gotta go now, Sherita. My friends are waiting for me," he said at last.

"Do you have to?"

"Yeah. If I don't practice every chance I get, I might not get on a soccer team in the spring. I can't practice in the winter and it's getting colder every day." Jerry hoped she would understand. You had to practice to be a soccer star.

"Well, okay, Jerry, if you have to," Sherita said, but she didn't sound happy about it.

Jerry wasn't either but he didn't know what to do. He hung the phone up slowly. He didn't even run to the playground.

CHAPTER **12**

Two weeks. Jerry wrote the two words in the margin of his science notebook. He hadn't been first at the playground in two weeks. He hadn't played soccer in two weeks except on the weekend and that wasn't enough. He had to solve Sherita's problem so he could get to the playground first.

He wondered if she had been scared of bears before she became a latchkey kid. He could tell her that there was nothing to be scared of, but he knew it wouldn't do any good. He remembered when he was in the second grade and his mother took him to swim classes at the Y. He had been afraid of the deep water. He had imagined there were monsters at the bottom. His mother and the instructor had told him not to be afraid, but it hadn't helped. Not until he had learned to swim and could skim over the top of the deep part had he gotten over his fear.

Once you do something like that, you aren't afraid anymore. But Sherita went home every day to the empty apartment, and still she was scared enough to call him up every day. Jerry had a feeling that Sherita was more lonesome than afraid. If she were really afraid, just talking to him on the phone wouldn't be enough to dispel her fear. He couldn't blame her for wanting someone to talk to. But all the same he couldn't be her company every day. He had to practice soccer.

His spelling book was open in front of him but he didn't see the page with the day's lesson on it. Instead, Jerry saw himself standing with one foot on a bear he had slain with a bow and arrow, a giant bear with long sharp teeth. Sherita was wearing a pink princess dress with a little gold crown over her braids. She would take his sword and touch him on each shoulder and the top of his head. "Arise, Sir Jerry," she would say.

There was a poke in his ribs. Jerry was annoyed.

Didn't Sherita know you didn't dub a knight in the ribs?

"Pssst, Jerry." It was Joel. He was poking Jerry with a pencil. "Get out your math book. Page sixty-six."

Jerry slid his book out of his desk. What had happened to spelling? He'd find out from Joel later. He was glad Mrs. Brent hadn't noticed his daydreaming. He tried to concentrate on his work for the rest of the afternoon.

Jerry was the third kid out of the school after the bell rang. He found a can to kick and started down his alley route.

The can skimmed along the alley, hardly touching the ground. Jerry burrowed down into his jacket as the wind whipped around a corner. Soon there would be snow on the ground. Jerry gave the can a sharp kick. It spurted forward.

"Another missile, soccer fans, an incredible kick by the one and only JJ," the announcer yelled over the roar of the crowd.

Spurred by the cheers, Jerry picked up speed and passed two boys throwing rocks. As Jerry whizzed by, he saw a small gray animal crouched in a doorway. A cornered rat, he thought. But he noticed it had a furry tail. Rats' tails, he knew, were stringy.

Jerry slowed down and stopped. He didn't want to go back. But the boys were throwing rocks at a kitten, a kitten that was smaller than a rat.

Jerry turned and went back. The boys were intent on their rock throwing and didn't pay any attention to him.

"Bull's-eye!" the taller one shouted.

The kitten yelped and spat as it tried to climb the door frame. But the metal frame was too slick for the kitten's claws and it slid down into a small heap of fur.

Jerry studied the boys. One was bigger than he was but the other was much smaller. He had never seen either of them before. He picked up his can and walked past them down the alley where he had just come. He set the can down on its end and made his plan.

First he took off his backpack and held it as he backed away. Then he ran towards the can and gave it a tremendous kick, a goal kick. Like a bullet the can streaked past the two boys and hit the brick wall in front of them. It bounced off the wall and hit the big boy smack in the chest.

Bull's-eye!

While the boys' attention was on the can, Jerry raced between them, scooped up the kitten, and stuck it into his backpack. Then he ran like the wind, like JJ, the world-famous soccer player.

Jerry could hear the two boys yelling at him as they realized what had happened and chased after him. But he wasn't worried. Nobody in the whole fourth grade and most of the fifth could catch him.

Jerry held the backpack against his chest and sprinted down the alley. The kitten didn't struggle. He hoped it had enough air.

The sounds of the two boys behind him grew fainter, then stopped. They had given up the chase. Jerry was glad because he had to wait for three cars to pass before he could cross the street.

In the apartment, he put the backpack on the kitchen floor and waited for the kitten to crawl out. But nothing in the backpack moved. Had the kitten suffocated? Jerry nudged the backpack with his foot. Still no movement. He picked up the end of the canvas and shook it gently. The kitten tumbled out onto the floor and looked around, blinking with surprise. It didn't seem to be afraid.

Jerry touched its head with one finger. It felt

soft. He stroked it. "You're a cute little guy," he told the kitten.

At the sound of his voice, the kitten looked up until it fell over backward. Jerry laughed. The kitten mewed.

"I'll bet you're hungry," Jerry said.

The kitten mewed again.

Jerry took a carton of milk out of the refrigerator and poured some in a bowl. But the milk felt awfully cold to him. Maybe he should warm it some like they do for babies. He poured about half a cup into a saucepan and put it on the stove to warm the way his dad had showed him. The kitten tried to follow him around the kitchen. It was the skinniest kitten Jerry had ever seen. Its bones stuck out in angles all over and its back sort of caved in on itself. He added some sugar to the milk.

How did you fatten up a kitten in a hurry? His mother always told him to eat his eggs because they would make him grow. Maybe the same thing was good for kittens. Jerry broke an egg in a bowl and beat it a little with a fork. Then he added the warm, sugared milk. He stuck his finger in and tasted it. Not bad. For a raw egg.

He put the bowl down in front of the kitten but

99

all it did was sit there and look at him. Jerry stuck his finger in the milk again and put it to the kitten's mouth. The kitten smelled his finger, then licked it. Jerry led it with his finger until its mouth was in the milk. The kitten began to lap the milk with tiny sounds as regular as the ticking of a watch.

The phone rang. Jerry talked to his mother as he watched the kitten. He didn't tell her about it. He knew their apartment building had a rule against pets. He didn't know what he was going to do, but one thing was certain: He wasn't going to put it back on the street to starve and be hurt by mean kids.

"Don't go to the playground today, Jerry," his mother said before she hung up. "I think it's going to rain. There have already been some sprinkles here."

"Aw, Mom," Jerry protested. But he did it half-heartedly because he didn't want to leave the kitten.

Jerry didn't tell Sherita about the kitten when she called, either. He listened to her talk about her project and even looked up turtle care in captivity for her without her asking.

But as soon as the kitten finished drinking its

100

egg-milk and began washing its paws, he hung up.

"I got to go now, Sherita," Jerry told her. "I've got some things to do."

"Are you going to the playground?"

"No, I have some things to do here."

"Okay, Jerry. Bye."

Jerry picked up the kitten. It hardly weighed anything and it was dirty. He couldn't even tell what color it was. It probably had fleas, too. The thought made him itch.

"Little guy, you've got to have a bath."

Jerry ran warm water in the bathroom sink. He added some of his mother's bubble stuff. The kitten didn't seem to mind the water or the bubbles. It batted the bubbles with its paws and looked surprised when they popped. It purred contentedly as he scrubbed its matted fur, which was still gray under all the dirt. Then he rinsed it again and again until the rinse water was clear. He dried the kitten carefully with a towel. Then he dried it more with his mother's hair dryer set on low. The kitten yawned and Jerry could see its sharp little teeth like tiny needles in its pink mouth.

Jerry tried to think what else a kitten needed. A bed. That was easy. A soft, old shirt wadded up

101

made a good one. And a cat box. Jerry remembered his grandmother's cat Marlowe used a box filled with kitty litter for its bathroom. He didn't have any kitty litter. Instead, he tore newspaper into confetti and put it in the box that had held comic books in the bottom of his closet.

As if that was what it had been waiting for, the kitten promptly jumped in the box and used it.

At least he didn't have to teach it how to do that, Jerry thought with relief. He made a ball of wadded up paper and played with the kitten until just before his mother came home.

When he heard her key in the lock, Jerry put the kitten in his closet with the box, its bed, a bowl of water, and some more egg-milk. His mother wouldn't find it before Saturday. The kitten was safe for now. But what was he going to do with the kitten when she found it?

CHAPTER 13

Everything would have been just fine, Jerry thought later, if his Aunt Louise hadn't called. She wanted to know if Jerry still had his sheep costume from the third-grade play. His cousin Billy had to be a sheep in his Sunday school Christmas pageant. When Jerry got out of the shower, his mother called him into the living room. She was holding the kitten.

"Look what I found, Jerry. I went in your closet to find a sheep suit and I found a kitten suit with the kitten still in it." She laughed at her joke.

Jerry didn't see anything to laugh about. He

waited to find out what his mother was going to do. She was stroking the kitten's ears and it was purring like a motorboat. Finally he couldn't stand it any longer. "Can I keep it?"

"It's a she. I'm sorry, Jerry. She's a nice cat and you know how much I like cats. But we can't have pets in our building."

"Why not? Nobody would know."

"Mr. Jones would find out sooner or later."

"How? How would he find out? Nobody would know but us."

She shook her head. "Sometimes the super has to come in when we aren't home. To fix the plumbing or something. It's too hard to find an apartment to get ourselves evicted over a cat. I'm sorry, Jerry, but the kitten will have to go. When we have our house we can have a cat."

"That won't help this kitten. Maybe I can find her another home."

"You can try. She can stay here until Saturday, but then you will have to take her to the animal shelter."

Jerry knew what that meant. Nobody would adopt a scrawny little kitten. The city had too many apartment buildings with no-pet rules. The animal shelter would put her to sleep. He couldn't

104

let that happen. "I'll find her a home first," he told his mother.

"I hope you can. She's a nice kitten. I'll ask at my office but I don't think it will do any good. One of the secretaries was trying to give away a whole litter of kittens a few weeks ago."

Jerry called all his friends. He was hoping they might know somebody who would take in a kitten.

"She's a good mouser," he told Ricky, who had a grandmother in the suburbs.

"I'll ask her," he promised. "But she already has three cats."

Joel called around, but everybody he knew lived in no-pet buildings, too. David's mother promised to ask at her office. John and Abe weren't home, but they probably couldn't help, either. Jerry stared at the telephone. What could he do? He hated the thought of taking the kitten to the shelter. The world was too full of kittens. Nobody would want an orphaned gray kitten as skinny as this one.

Jerry turned on the TV. There must be somebody in the world who would want a cute little kitten. He flipped through the channels. A cooking program. "Just pour it in and watch the bubbles form. Look at those nice bubbles. . . ." Jerry turned the dial. "But Ronald, Millicent knows about us . . ."

That sounds like one of Mr. Feeney's programs, Jerry thought.

Then Jerry had an inspiration. Mr. Feeney! He lived all alone. The kitten would be great company for him!

Jerry got out the phone book and looked up Feeney. He found a B. F. Feeney at the right address. Jerry dialed the number.

"Hello," Mr. Feeney answered.

"Hi, Mr. Feeney. This is Jerry Johnson. Um, how are you?" Jerry asked. Now that he was actually talking to Mr. Feeney, Jerry found it hard to just say "Do you want a cat?"

"I still have a tickle in my throat," Mr. Feeney said.

Jerry thought his voice sounded sort of croaky. "Are you taking your medicine?"

"Five times a day," Mr. Feeney said.

"Um, that's too bad, I mean that's good. Mr. Feeney, would you like a cat?" Jerry blurted, "I mean a kitten?"

"A kitten? I sure would. We always had cats on the farm. Dotty and I had cats after we were married. But after she died I moved to this building.

No pets are allowed here," Mr. Feeney said, "except fish and birds. I had to give my cat away."

"Who did you give it to?" Jerry asked hopefully.

"I gave Minnie to a friend."

"Do you think your friend would like another cat?" Jerry explained about the kitten.

"I'm sorry, boy. They moved to California a year or two ago." Mr. Feeney was silent for a few moments. Then he said, "Reckon it was more nearly five years ago. Time gets away from me."

"Well, thanks anyway, Mr. Feeney," Jerry said.

At school the next day Jerry asked everybody he knew, including teachers. The answer was the same. The people who could have pets already had them. "You'd think I could find somebody who had just lost a pet," Jerry told Joel.

When Sherita called that afternoon, he didn't even try to get off the phone. He wasn't going to the playground. He needed the afternoon to find a home for the kitten. He was running out of time. Tomorrow he would have to take the kitten to the shelter.

He felt something soft touch his ankle. He looked down. The kitten was rolling around at his feet, playing with the strap on his shoe. She didn't seem worried. She didn't know what was in store for her.

"Don't you think so?" Sherita asked.

"Huh?"

"Jerry, you aren't paying attention," Sherita scolded him.

"Um, I'm sorry Sherita. I was thinking."

"What? What were you thinking, Jerry?"

Suddenly Jerry remembered something. Something Sherita had told him a long time ago in her first phone call when she told him she was afraid of bears. She liked cats. She had told him that she liked cats. Jerry brightened. It was worth a try.

"Say, Sherita, do you know anybody who has a pet?"

"You mean like a dog?"

"Yeah. Or a cat."

"I know two people with dogs. Mrs. Falzoni lives on the floor above us. She has a poodle named Muffet. Little Miss Muffet is her real name. She's white and wears little red bows in her hair. Mrs. Falzoni lets me pet her when I see them in the elevator. And Mr. Cole has a Doberman named King. People are afraid of King because

108

he's a Doberman but Mr. Cole says he's a pus-
sycat."

Jerry felt his excitement growing as Sherita
talked. He couldn't believe his luck. Sherita lived
in an apartment building that allowed pets.

"But I don't think I know anybody with a cat.
Cats probably don't have to be walked like dogs.
So I never see them. Why do you want to know?"

"Oh, I was just wondering." Jerry switched the
conversation to turtles.

"I have to go now," he said finally. "Um, could
I come over Saturday and see you, Sherita? I
could see your turtle, too."

"You want to come here? To see me?" Her
voice went up and ended in a little squeal.

"Um, well, I thought I would. Since it's Saturday."

"I'll have to ask my mother. I'll call you back
tonight."

Jerry didn't think he could wait that long.

Sherita called back after supper.

"My mom said you can come, Jerry. What
time?"

They decided on ten o'clock. "See you tomorrow, Sherita," Jerry said.

"I think I've found you a home," he told the

kitten as he hung up. The kitten mewed and tried to climb his pants leg. Jerry scooped it up and put it on his bed. The kitten curled up and went to sleep. She wasn't worried about her future, Jerry thought. She trusted Jerry to take care of her.

Jerry went to sleep with the kitten snuggled under the covers with him. He dreamed that he was playing soccer. Tank's team were sheep, Jerry's were cats. Sherita was a cheerleader but instead of a pom-pom, she carried the kitten. As he dribbled downfield, the soccer ball turned into a can. Sherita ran into the goal with the kitten and said, "I scored, Jerry. Look, I scored, too!"

CHAPTER **14**

The bus doors closed with a *whoosh.* Jerry hugged the shoe box against him. He hoped the kitten would be all right in it. He had put his old shirt in for her to lie on and punched air holes in one side. The kitten mewed softly.

"Ssshhh, kitty," he whispered. He glanced around, but nobody seemed to notice. He didn't know if pets were allowed on a bus. His mother had said it was all right as long as the kitten was in a box. "Don't stay too long," she'd said when he left. "Be home by four. Dad said he'd try to call then."

Sherita opened the door before he had time to ring the bell. "I knew it was you," she said. "I heard the elevator bell and I knew it was you."

Today she had ladybug barrettes on her braids. Her green T-shirt had horses galloping across the middle. A tall woman in jeans and a yellow sweater stood behind her.

"Mama, this is Jerry. Jerry, this is my mama, Mrs. Thomas."

"Hello, Jerry." She smiled at him. "Sherita tells me that you help her with her schoolwork sometimes. That's so nice of you."

"Yes, ma'am, Mrs. Thomas. I helped her with her turtle project."

"Do you want to see my turtle, Jerry?" Sherita asked.

"Um, sure."

She held out a lumpy playclay turtle. Jerry could see that art was not Sherita's thing. "That's a . . . uh . . . great turtle, Sherita," he said.

"What's in the box?" Sherita poked at the box Jerry held under his arm. "It has air holes in it. Is it alive, Jerry? Is it a real turtle?"

"That's a good guess. But, no, it's not a turtle." He didn't know how to tell Sherita and her mother about the kitten.

112

But he didn't have to. Sherita poked at the box again and the top fell off. The kitten blinked sleepily at them.

"Oh, a little kitten!" Sherita squealed.

Mrs. Thomas didn't say anything. Jerry stole a quick look at her. She didn't look mad or anything. She looked interested.

Jerry hoped the kitten would yawn. It was so cute when it did that. The kitten looked at him and, as if it were reading his mind, it yawned and stretched.

"Oh, look at him yawn!" Sherita said.

"Her. He's a her," Jerry corrected.

"Is she your kitten, Jerry? Can I hold her?"

"You can hold her. But she's not my kitten. I mean, she would be but pets aren't allowed in my building. I was hoping you could keep her."

He looked at Mrs. Thomas. She was smiling at the kitten but she still didn't say anything.

"She's no trouble. She uses a box and she doesn't eat much. She even likes being washed. She needs fattening up. She was real skinny when I found her." Jerry told them how he had saved her from the boys. "Those boys would have killed her," he finished.

Sherita picked up the kitten. She cuddled it

under her chin. The kitten reached up with a soft paw and patted Sherita's cheek.

"You don't have to walk her or anything like that," Jerry pointed out. "She's a real good kitten. I'll help you make a litter box. I already know how. And . . ."

The kitten batted at the ladybug on one of Sherita's pigtails.

". . . and she'd be real good company for Sherita after school."

Mrs. Thomas laughed. "Okay, Jerry, okay. You don't have to sell me the kitten. She's already sold herself. And I think you are a hero for bringing her to Sherita," she added softly.

"Um, what are you going to name her?" he asked Sherita.

"Gracie. I'm going to call her Gracie."

"Why Gracie?" Jerry asked.

"Because she's gray, silly."

CHAPTER **15**

Jerry sniffed the air as he ran home from school. It smelled funny, sort of frosted. The sky was a strange sort of paper white with a brighter light behind it, like a Japanese lantern. Jerry sent a can spinning ahead of him. It was a fat tin can that had probably once held beans or corn.

He didn't have to worry about Sherita holding him up anymore. Since she'd gotten Gracie she only called him up at night sometimes to talk. She reported every little thing Gracie did. The time she got tangled up in Sherita's hair ribbons. The time she ran from the vacuum cleaner and Sherita

115

couldn't find her for almost an hour. Jerry bet he could write a book about Gracie.

The can shot across the last street. Jerry was glad to be home. He wished those clouds would go away. He was sure they meant rain or snow. Either way they meant no soccer unless they held off for another two hours.

But to his mother, the clouds were the same as snow or rain. "Don't go to the playground today, Jerry," she told him.

"Jeeps, Mom, why not?"

"Because it's either going to snow or rain."

"Not for a while," he protested.

"Jerry."

"Okay, Mom." Jerry hung up and turned on the TV. A cartoon about a pink mouse was on. All the other mice beat it up until it put on its magic cape. Then it became a super mouse that could do anything. Jerry yawned. It was a boring cartoon. His feet itched to run and kick a ball.

It was cold in the apartment. Jerry checked the heat. It was on and the thermostat was on its usual setting. Jerry wondered why he still felt cold. It must be the strange white light coming in through the windows. He changed the channel and found Dr. Monroe in a lab with Dr. James Turner. Dr.

Turner was wearing a long black cape. "I have longed to tell you . . ." he said as he took a step toward Dr. Monroe.

"Yuck," Jerry thought. "Mr. Feeney's favorite program."

Jerry switched again to the educational channel. A nature program about the American desert was on. A snake slithered across the TV screen.

That was better. Jerry sprawled on the sofa. The desert made the room seem a little warmer, but not much.

Jerry watched a sidewinder sidle through the sand. Yucko. Suddenly, dazzling silver light shot through the room. Jerry jumped. It must have been a transformer blowing out somewhere, he thought.

Next a beaded Gila monster oozed along the TV screen. It gave Jerry the creeps. He shivered.

Light flashed at the window. This time Jerry caught a glimpse of the quicksilver, root-shaped light. It was lightning. A drumroll of thunder confirmed it.

Jerry wasn't afraid of thunder and lightning. But the next flash lit up an eerie scene outside his window. Instead of rain, he saw jillions of snowflakes falling silently from the heavy clouds. Jerry ran to the window. The ground was already covered with white. It must have been snowing silently ever since he'd come home.

But snow and lightning? Jerry had never heard of it happening at the same time.

He pulled the curtains together and turned on a lamp. That was better, he thought. But a minute later there was a giant flash and a deafening roar. Both the TV and the lamp went out with a loud snap.

Jerry opened the curtains and stared out of the window. A thick curtain of snow hung from the dull white sky. Snow iced the ledges and windowsills of the apartment building across the street and whitened the rooftops almost to the peaks. There was no color anywhere. The red stop sign at the corner was whited out. The neon lights had been blown out. The world from his window was all gray, black, and white. Jerry thought it looked as though some monster had sucked all the color out of the world. Every few seconds lightning streaked the sky with silver.

It was the scariest, most beautiful sight Jerry had ever seen.

He thought of Sherita. He bet she was scared with the lights out and the weather gone crazy. He wondered why she didn't call him. He sort of wished she would. Maybe he should call her. He wasn't scared, but he wouldn't mind talking to somebody himself.

He dialed her number.

"Hi, Sherita, this is Jerry."

"Hi, Jerry."

There was a pause. Then Jerry said, "Did you look outside?"

"Yes. It's snowing and lightning," she said matter-of-factly. She didn't seem a bit afraid. "I thought it was supposed to rain when it lightninged."

"I thought so, too. It sure is weird weather. Um, Sherita, you're not scared, are you?"

"No. Are you?"

Jerry thought about it. He had been. A little. He wasn't now. But he didn't want to hang up yet. "No. I'm not scared. What are you doing?"

"I'm sitting in a chair with Gracie. We've been eating cookies and I'm reading a story to her. Would you like to hear it?"

"Uh, yeah, I guess so."

"Okay. It's called *Snowbear.* Once upon a time there was a little bear who didn't want to hibernate like all the other bears. 'Why do I have to sleep all winter in a moldy old cave? It's boring. Why can't I stay up and play in the snow?' he asked." Sherita read the little bear's part in a high little voice.

" 'Because you're a bear and bears hibernate all winter,' said his father." She made the father's voice gruff.

" 'Go to sleep, son,' said his mother." Sherita read the mother's voice in her own normal voice.

"When his parents began to snore, he tiptoed out of the cave. Snowflakes fell on the little bear. . . ." Jerry's thoughts began to wander.

"Suddenly there was a loud rumbling, growling sound." Sherita made a low growl and went on reading. "The little bear stopped making a snowball. 'What was that?' he asked his friend the fox."

" 'It was your stomach growling.' "

Jerry laughed. She sounded so funny growling. She didn't seem to be afraid of bears anymore. He wondered if she had bear barrettes on her braids.

"Soon the little bear was snoring, too, and he slept soundly all winter long. The end. Did you like that story, Jerry?"

He did but he was glad his friends couldn't see him listening to a second grader reading a baby book to him over the telephone. "I liked the special effects best," he said.

"The what?"

"Your growling. And that reminds me, I'm hungry, too. And I can't hibernate because I have to study spelling."

"Gracie wants to tell you good-bye. 'Bye, Jerry,' " said a little voice that was supposed to sound like a cat voice.

"Um, bye, Gracie." Jerry hung up and looked out the window. It was still snowing, but the thunder had dwindled to a distant rumble and the lightning was fainter. But the power was still off and it was getting dark. He couldn't watch TV.

Without the TV on, the apartment seemed colder. Jerry put his jacket back on and thought of Mr. Feeney. He probably had on at least three or four coats and several blankets and quilts with only his eyes uncovered so he could watch his programs. Then he remembered that the power was off. Mr. Feeney couldn't watch TV. Jerry wondered what he was doing without his programs.

Jerry thought maybe he should call him. But Mr. Feeney had a telephone. He could call somebody if he wanted to. But he wouldn't, because he wouldn't want to spend the money on a call. Jerry knew he had to do it. He opened the phone book.

Jerry dialed the number. Mr. Feeney picked it up in the middle of the first ring. "Hello? Who's this?"

"It's Jerry, Mr. Feeney. You remember, Jerry Johnson?"

"Oh, yes, I remember. How are you?"

"I'm fine, Mr. Feeney."

"Did you find a home for the cat?"

"I sure did." Jerry told him about Sherita.

"I'm glad to hear it."

There was a pause. Then Jerry said, "Um, Mr. Feeney, is your TV out?"

"It sure is," Mr. Feeney said. "It went off right at the end of 'Hospital Hearts,' just as Dr. Monroe discovered an electronic bug in her stethoscope. I can't wait to find out who put it there."

"I bet it was Arlene Alewine," Jerry said.

"Why would she do that?"

"To get something bad on Dr. Monroe because she wants Michael."

"No, Michael disappeared last week. I think it was his ex-wife Carlotta."

They discussed who might have done it and why. Then Jerry said, "I guess I better hang up now, Mr. Feeney. Um, would you like to go to a soccer game with my dad and me sometime?"

There was a silence. Then Mr. Feeney said, "A soccer game?"

"Yeah. We go on Saturdays when my dad is here." Jerry was beginning to think he'd made Mr. Feeney mad or something.

Jerry waited while Mr. Feeney had a coughing spell. He wondered if Mr. Feeney had on the scarves that made him look like a turtle. "A soccer game, then?"

"Yes, sir."

Mr. Feeney blew his nose. Jerry wondered if he were laughing or crying or having an allergic reaction. He waited politely.

Finally Mr. Feeney said, "Well, I believe I'd like that, Jerry. I do believe I would, weather permitting."

"Okay, Mr. Feeney. See you then."

"Yes, Jerry. I will see you then. Thank you, son."

Jerry hung up. Why had he done that? Mr. Feeney was the last person he wanted to go to a soccer game with. Mr. Feeney probably didn't even like soccer. But he'd sounded like he really wanted to go. Or that he was glad he had been asked. Maybe that was it.

Jerry's mom would probably be home soon. Jerry wondered what they would have for supper since they couldn't use the stove. He hoped she wouldn't decide on salad. Maybe she would order out for pizza. He wondered if Pizza Palace would deliver with all the snow in the streets. Maybe they could heat a can of Sloppy Joe over a candle. Or would it take more than one candle?

He bet even Joel didn't know the answer to that. Jerry would tell him tomorrow at school. But maybe there wouldn't be any school. Maybe everybody would have to stay home. The playground would be piled with snow. Jerry thought about all the things he and his friends could do in the snow. They could build a giant snow fort. They could build the biggest snow fort in the neighborhood, or even the world.